Soft Boys Play Hard

Kon Blacke

DDP
DEEP DESIRES PRESS
Winnipeg, Canada

Soft Boys Play Hard

Saturday, July 24th

The techno music thumped, *doof doof doof,* right through my chest, making my voice go funny whenever I shouted. So awesome. The sweating crowd heaved all around me, intertwined, most kissing, their passion filling the air as much as the smoke produced by the fog machines. Colored lights flashed, lasers too. I bloody well loved it. 'Cause *this* was *Badda-Bings*, my dad's gay gentlemen's club, on a Saturday night, and I couldn't think of any other place I'd rather be.

My name's Jake Brock-Wilson, and this here's my story once I came of age, as they say. 'Cause yeah, tonight the club was packed to the rafters all thanks to me.

This was my party.

My eighteenth.

Yet, despite loving the attention I got, sometimes even from the cute waiters who wore nothing but glittery, brightly colored G-stings, cheeky smiles, and nothing else, I only had eyes for one man.

My heart was his too.

All night, Larry held me like I was the only one there, the only one who mattered. My heart fluttered every time he looked into my eyes. Every time he caressed my back while holding me. Every time he smiled.

'Cause I knew all of that was just for me.

Then, like a fairy tale really, on the stroke of midnight Larry pressed his lips against mine, sending me into a spin. I was glad he was holding me tightly. Otherwise, I knew I would have fallen flat on my ass onto the dance floor, my knees suddenly going weak. My breath was taken from me, but that's only 'cause my already fluttering heart became lodged in my throat.

His kiss…no, *our kiss*, quickly deepened.

There was a hunger about it from the both of us, complete with wandering hands and everything. Hands that wandered lower. Larry soon cupped my butt firmly, keeping me held into to his massive bulk.

I fucking loved it.

When parted with our kiss, breathless, licking my numb lips from our passion, sweating from the rush too, needing more, he said dreamily, "I gotta say, I love how I've gotta pick ya up so that we can pash."

His words cut through the noise of the music and the din of the crowd 'cause they spoke directly to my soul. And as far as I was concerned, that was always open for him, no matter what.

Without thought, and grinding myself against him, feeling safe, warm, and loved enough to do so, hardening too, I replied, "Larry, I so love that you can pick me up and hold me. It's everything to me. But don't you think it's now time for you to have your way with me, now that I'm legal?"

Larry smiled from ear to ear. "Hell yeah, I've been waitin' for this moment for so long, gotta tell ya."

"Me too. And I can't wait anymore either." Funnily enough, I trembled with anticipation and a touch of nerves then. Good nerves. I also felt myself get warm, especially through my cheeks to my neck when I added, "Let's get outta here so you can fuck my brains out—I need your dick in me, Larry, no lie!"

He didn't reply, only kept grinning, looking hungry like a wolf, an expression that went to his sparkling blue eyes, beyond that even. And yeah, that sure did reach to my soul and then some, 'cause my dick went rock hard, uncomfortably so. Jeez! I was panting for him, I really was.

What's more, he didn't let me go either!

Larry carried me easily across the dance floor towards the exit like I was his blushing bride, me giggling as I hung my arms around his shoulders, people parting in his wake, smiling, patting us both on our backs.

"Go git it on, lads!" one guy screamed nearest me, causing others to add their encouragement until it became a chorus.

So good.

'Cause yeah, our love for each other had been building up for so long, weeks now, I was at boiling point. Truly. We'd spent every waking moment together for just as much time too; I quit my old office job with Mister Anderson and now worked for Larry as his office clerk at his reinvigorated investigation company.

And 'cause of how we were, and not leaving any doubt about it, everyone knew what was going to happen next between us. I couldn't be happier, not even if the sky fell to try and ruin our moment. 'Cause even if such a disaster did happen, the world thrown back into the Stone Age or something, I'm sure Larry would still do me in some cave in the dark while everyone else panicked.

I'd be fine with that too.

During the drive to our hotel room, the one my dad had paid for as part of my birthday present, I couldn't help but stare lovingly at Larry. All the way there, no less. I also touched him the same way, my attention on his inside leg more than anywhere else.

"You're makin' me harder, ya know that?" Larry stated, obviously trying his best to concentrate on driving through the busy streets, other cars lights blurring before us 'cause of a light drizzle.

"It's my intention, I'm sure you realize." I was being cheeky, but I didn't care.

I wanted him.

He chuckled. "Ya so gonna get it, Jake-y."

"Again, my intention," I replied giggling, trying to be coy but failing.

Seriously, I was like a salivating dog, begging for any little treat from him, a smile, wink, nod, anything, I'd become that horny. And aside from my own hard-on making me ache, tingling all over with my lust, from what I felt of his, when we got into our room, I would be getting the biggest treat of them all.

Jeez, I wanted him so bad.

The wait had been long enough. Too long. I'd soon be gagging for it, no damn doubt. And gag for it I would.

Bloody awesome.

When we were *finally* at the hotel, car valet parked and the both of us checked in, Larry carried me across the threshold into our room up on one of the top floors—one of the penthouses, I believed.

The place was huge!

Larry put me down gently, both of us beaming smiles. But before I could worship him as I knew I would, my big and handsome bara man, oh my, I *had* to take a second to soak in where I'd found myself.

Explore it too.

Not only was the room massive, it was lavish in every way possible. From the extravagant furnishings, to fine cushions, patterned rugs, champagne waiting for us, chocolates too, to the size of the TV and tub, it was amazing. Dad went all out for Larry and me. Wow. In fact, the tub had its own TV we could watch while soaking in it. Even the loo was fancy—the kind that cleans your butt for you in various different ways, depending on the buttons pressed.

Double wow!

"I don't think I belong in here," I admitted.

Larry, always reassuring, said, "Ya belong anywhere, ya do."

"Oh?" I was momentarily confused. "What makes you say that?"

"'Cause ya with me, that's why," he stated matter-of-factly, shrugging but adding a reassuring wink. I couldn't argue with that. "So why don't'cha come here and give me some of that lovin' ya been promisin'." And with that, he unbuttoned his shirt and slipped it off his massive shoulders, quick as a flash.

I almost fainted at the sight of what was revealed.

Larry's pecs alone, massive mounds of rippling tanned muscle capped by beautifully pinkish-brown nipples, hard and getting harder, were worth the cost of the room. But I knew I'd be seeing more. So much more! At the same time, and because I'd been waiting for so long, I honestly felt like a pauper who'd been invited to a feast; I didn't know where to start!

As such, I stood there awestruck, quivering with delight, eyes wide and unable to process anything 'cause his presence affected me that much.

I mean, to see Larry without his shirt on, sure was something as my gaze wandered all over him. I gulped as I did so, feeling my extremities tingle, my dick leak into my undies, soaking them I'm sure, and my heart pound and pound. 'Cause jeez, even his arms, especially his biceps, were also a wonderland waiting to be discovered—they were so bulky and hard I wanted to touch them…no, I wanted to do more than that.

I wanted to kiss them.

Without delay, not even thinking about it any further, I rushed to him, feeling myself stir even more, butterflies rising. I yearned, ached to the point of delightful hurt as soon as I touched his bare skin and caressed him lovingly. Larry was so warm. Smelt great too; that combination cologne he wore (which was still his secret) and his musky manliness all rolled into one intoxicated me.

Larry was a veritable assault to the senses.

The best kind.

With quivering lips close to his nipples, I whispered, "I want to kiss you all over, your nips, your pecs, your biceps, your abs, all of you."

Larry groaned. "Do it, please! Worship me, Jake-y!"

And yeah, he *was* a god to be worshiped—*my* god—for sure. "I so will. Now get yourself on that bed. This is just the start of it."

Larry obeyed.

I was on top of him within a trembling breath. His bulk beneath me was more than a comfort, but I didn't waste any more time to simply stare. I got to it.

Licking my lips, wetting them, I kissed his nipples, soon rolling my tongue around them, leaving them wet, loving that I did. Loving even more how he also quivered, moaned too, 'cause of what I did to him.

"Mhmm, yeah!" he said, as breathless as I was. "That's good."

As I worked my mouth, rubbing myself against him as I did so, crotch against crotch, rising to the delirious heights, warming as well, he whispered, "Sniff my pits. Get me really hard, Jake-y!"

Larry moved his arms so they were above his head, exposing his armpits for me, those shaved wonders like deep crevices of delight between the massive forms of his pecs and posterior shoulder muscles.

"That's sooo hot," I said, crawling up him so I could do as he asked, also loving that the things which seemed to turn him on were making me feel giddy with lust as well.

I loved smelling Larry as much as I could. Now, and

with my nose where he desired it, where I did too, I was getting his full pungency. But I didn't stop with smelling. No. I kissed and licked him there too, savoring the tangy sweetness that welcomed me.

My tongue tingled as much as the rest of me.

He was soon wet from my efforts there, his manly flavor dissipating because of my attention. But I didn't stop. I went to his other armpit. Again, his musk was riper and more arousing than the rest of him there.

I savored it so much, moaning my arousal.

Soon, I wanted to kiss and lick him all over, all of his muscles in turn, I really did, including the bulging mass I could feel between his legs.

That would be my reward for doing my best for him.

But not yet.

Larry had other ideas.

"Kiss me!" he said. "Lemme taste myself off ya lips."

And as it was asked, I did so. I kissed him, deeply and with passion that could have only come 'cause of the build-up we'd shared already. I was in his mouth with my tongue as much as I'd been in his pits, feeling safe and secure lying on him, draped over him really, his muscles heaving with his rapidly increasing breathing.

It was amazing to experience.

The kiss we shared, felt to our souls, lived and cherished lasted forever. A wonderful forever ending all too quickly, as far as I was concerned. I moaned, wanting more.

I got my wish.

We kissed and kissed again, my emotions and my lust increasing exponentially while our tongues connected us in such a special way. By the time I parted I was a quivering, wonderful disaster. Sweating too.

"Oh…Larry!" I managed through numb lips wet with my affection for him.

"Take me clothes off," he said, voice sounding as wolfish as his expression now. "Smell me everywhere. Kiss me. Do ya thing! Make me so horny for ya I won't be able to stand the madness that'll follow."

I nodded.

A blink of an eye later, I removed his pants.

The sight of his bulge almost sent me into a carnal spin.

Oh. My. God!

The wet patch too.

"You're…you're so *big*," I said, not just referring to his muscles.

I couldn't help but smile. Feel anxious and desire in equal measure too. Yeah, I'd soon have his monster dick inside me, in my mouth and my ass in turn, but I needed it to be so.

Really needed it.

What good was a thirsty bottom boy without his man's dick inside him, anyway? And yep, it's a good thing I'd been preparing myself for this moment with an amply sized dildo I'd bought online a few weeks ago. I don't know how I was going to take Larry, otherwise.

I didn't want to disappoint—him or me.

He said, "Yeah. Ya do *that* to me, Jake-y."

I wasted no more time. I took down his undies with trembling hands, his dick slapping against his stomach as I did so, leaking, throbbing, and getting harder and harder because I'd exposed it for me to enjoy.

His dick *was* huge—a good nine inches of veiny meat, if not more.

But before I could do as he wanted, as I wanted as well no doubt, I sucked in a deep breath, one that hitched within my throat. It took me a moment to compose myself after that, unable to do anything but stare wide-eyed at the sight of him sprawled out on the soft, luxurious bedding before me. My Larry. Mine.

Far out, I loved him being fully naked. All that muscle everywhere, the bulk of him I could get lost within, even before he'd wrap me in his love, as I knew he would.

"You're uncut," I blurted, again breathlessly, trembling even more with growing lust.

I kind of felt relief he was like me down there. Although, there were differences between us; his foreskin pretty much revealed all of his swollen knob, like a gift half unwrapped of its own accord, unlike mine which kept me covered no matter how hard I got 'cause I had a lot longer one.

I wanted to lick and kiss him all over.

As such, I grabbed it, holding it up, feeling its warmth and weight—it was a unique feeling holding another man's instead of my own, I admitted. I also liked it…no, adored it.

What a beautiful thing he had.

"You know what?" I said with more intakes of breaths, stomach doing that whole fluttering thing over and over. "I reckon I could hang the contents of my wardrobe off of your hard-on."

Larry blushed. "Then how 'bout ya worship it before I cum 'cause I'm lookin' at such beauty and I dunno how much longer I can last."

He thought I was beautiful? Wow. I thought he was too.

"For you, I'll do anything."

I moved so I could do as he'd asked.

The scent of him, his pubes, balls, his dick most of all, was so alluring, intoxicating, and even stronger than I'd smelt in his pits. It sent me into a spin it was that good, it really did. I then sniffed under his foreskin once I pulled it back fully.

What a rush.

I got even more giddy, closer to the edge and the point of no return, really. The musky, almost woody odor of him was ripe and full, the cause of my fervor. If his pits were like savoring delicacies on a plate, his dick was like a smorgasbord sprawled out across a table.

"Mhmm…" I said as I gave him what we both desired.

I kissed and sucked, saliva dripping, around his knob, getting into every nook and cranny to taste him as much as smell him. I felt myself approaching climax as I did so, unable to help myself.

Larry must have caught on that I was close.

"Get ya clothes off, lemme worship ya for a moment."

I got up off him, missing the feeling of him being in my mouth already. How it made my jaw ache and my mouth tingle 'cause all his pre-cum washed right through it, tangy and tasty.

By the time I got my trousers off, hands trembling with anticipation, I felt the inevitable shudder through the depths of me to my balls. I shuddered again with a gasp that time. Then, over and over, I felt the inevitable release.

Shit!

I'd jizzed myself before I could even get my undies off for Larry. I collapsed, my knees giving way underneath me because of my orgasm.

Larry caught me.

I felt myself burn with embarrassment as the remnants of the rush I'd felt still washed through me. "I'm…sorry."

And I felt what I said genuinely.

Larry moved so he could look me in the eyes. "What are ya sorry for?" he questioned.

I could only stare at him, unable to quantify my feelings, my disappointment that I'd shot my wad before we even got down to the good stuff. Before he fucked me as I'd been wanting him to.

Larry didn't seem perturbed, 'cause after his reassurance, he gently pulled down my underwear, peeling them away. A sticky, stringy mass of cum stuck everywhere, including within my pubes, greeted him.

More flushing of heat through my cheeks to my neck and beyond resulted. Why had I got myself so worked up? Then again, could I be blamed for that when Larry was just too irresistible?

He then did the most surprising thing. I couldn't help it; I let out a little yelp of joy as he gently moved me so I was now lying down, him over me. I was about to question him, when, and with a shudder of delight and disbelief added for good measure, he began to lick up my mess.

He ate my prematurely ejaculated cum, lapped it up like a puppy would his dinner. He savored it. Loved it. All, no doubt, because it was mine.

I became overwhelmed again.

"Thank you…" was all I could utter as I felt myself get hard again.

Larry, once he'd cleaned me up properly, my dick and balls dripping with his saliva instead of my eagerness, came up so we were nose to nose.

I had a thought.

With my insides going all funny again, butterflies and everything, I whispered, "Spit my cum into my mouth! Dribble it in. Wet my tongue with it and your own saliva before you kiss me." I began trembling with excitement again, loving what we'd already done together 'cause it more than met my expectations. Way more. "Treat me like I'm your dirty boy who's horny for you again, Larry."

He smiled. "Ya are my dirty boy."

"I so am."

"And my good boy," he added. He looked down at my raging boner that'd found me again. "My very good boy."

I opened my mouth wider for him.

He hooked both of his thumbs into the corners of my lips, keeping me open. Not that I wanted to close my mouth. Still, with that and his weight pressed on top of me, I was at his whim.

Jeez, I loved that idea.

Larry opened his mouth. The jizz he hadn't swallowed so he could talk to me, his saliva combined with it too, dribbled from his mouth in a thick strand to go where I wanted it to go, right onto my tongue. The tang and salt, bitter and sweet too, overwhelmed my taste buds.

I writhed underneath him.

Moaned as well.

I liked the taste of myself, I ate it often enough, but combined with Larry's drool, it was even better. More fluid. What's more, and because of his own arousal, he produced a lot of spit. It filled my mouth.

But I didn't want to swallow.

I wanted to kiss him, share what we both produced with each other in one passionate, unbelievable kiss. No sooner had I wrapped my arms around him kiss me he did, as I kissed him.

It was awesome!

We were connected again, this time the glue between us something unique; something that'd been a mistake on my part but turned into something wonderful.

I adored him for what he did.

We became intertwined, rolling around, moaning and groaning, as we became each other's world. I wouldn't want it any other way. Not a chance in hell.

By the time he was above me again, I was sweating. Hard as a rock too. As was he.

"Can I put it inside ya now, Jake-y?"

"I thought you'd never ask—and you sure can."

Larry reached over, getting the lube and applying it liberally to where it mattered. As he did so, anticipation building again, I clawed at the bed, arching my back, yearning beyond belief for what would follow.

Jeez, I needed him.

I was soon underneath his bulk again, Larry's body blocking out everything but the sight of his sweat running down his muscles in rivulets.

He wore a lust-filled smile too, one that drove me crazy.

Quickly, Larry shuffled into position between my wide-open legs, everything within me quivering with expectation. Trembling with my love for him.

Larry held me again, like I was the only one in existence.

I moaned deep from my throat as I felt a pressure at the perfect spot where I desired him. Then a moment of pause, a gasp of time for the both of us before he gently pushed himself into me.

"Holy shit!" I hissed through my teeth, arching my back even more.

The *pop* that followed as his swollen knob entered me, as I surrendered my body to him, giving him everything of myself, almost blew my mind. My head spun. I writhed, trying to get comfortable. I needed a moment, indicating to him that I did.

He gave it.

When comfortable enough I nodded, giving him my permission to continue. He pushed even more, still gentle, still caring, still holding me. I was his, from now until the stars winked out in the heavens and the dark that resulted would envelop our intertwined bodies.

"So hot, bein' inside ya, Jake-y," Larry said, his eyes watery.

He was feeling it as much as I was.

"Yeah, it's good to finally…have you there."

Larry pushed again, that time with more intent, seating himself. I shuddered, almost bucking but managing to control myself as my ass opened up wider for him, stretching me.

It hurt.

Fucking hell did it hurt. I yelled, eyes watering, mouth open, panting, quivering, as I experienced his connection with me, as it should be. As I…no, as *we* wanted it.

But Larry stopped, concern etched onto his blushed expression.

"No! Keep going!" I begged, because despite my pain, underneath all that, there was a comfort. "Keeeep goooing!"

The soothing feeling, to my surprise, quickly took over and calmed me.

After that, Larry gained his rhythm and I gained mine, assisting him, pushing up when he thrust down. We were one. Truly.

I don't know how long Larry stayed within me, holding me, kissing me as I kissed him, but I was numb all over by the time he began grunting and shuddering with more intent.

"I'm gonna…cum!" he declared, baring his teeth, nostrils flaring, breathing becoming deeper.

"Give it to me," I said, feeling his heat and his love. "Shoot your load deep into my ass, my handsome bara man! Fill me up!"

"Yeah, Jake-y."

And Larry came.

It was so adorable. Not only did he do that whole 'O' face expression as he blew his load into me, he squinted, cheeks flushed, and everything shook, his muscles most of all. It was like an earthquake rippled through him, my ass the epicenter. So awesome to witness and feel, for sure.

I pulled him closer as he collapsed onto me, our sweat mingling as much as our love. The best part of all was the fact I could feel him let go inside me. So much better than anything else I'd experienced. Worth the wait, above all else, no damn doubt.

Larry was so good it took me ages to cool, but I knew it would take longer to not be so sore. I didn't care. How I felt was the reminder of what we'd shared, his mark upon me, and I wouldn't change it for anything.

When we both stopped panting, still sweating, Larry, between tender soft kisses all over my face and lips, whispered, "Thanks, Jake-y. That was so good."

"It so bloody well was," I agreed.

A grin found his lips. "Are ya satisfied?"

After he said that, I realized I was still hard, rubbing myself against him to prove it while he remained within me. "I could do with more, if you're up for it."

"Good." Another wet and sexy kiss. "Then I want you to get on top of me so you can push my pecs together and fuck me between 'em, Jake-y! Then I want ya to squirt ya jizz onto my face—I wanna taste your boy juice again."

That was so hot, I went all warm everywhere. "Can I lick my jizz off you so we can share another cum-filled kiss?"

"For sure, ya can."

I stirred even more, getting harder than before. "Then let's do it."

It took a moment for us to get into position, but when we were, me sitting on him so I was in the perfect position to slip my dick between his massive pecs, grabbing them, I felt his jizz leaking out of my ass, dribbling onto his abs.

"I'm also gonna lick up your mess coming out of me as well," I stated, smiling knowingly, feeling as naughty as I'd ever felt.

So wickedly good.

Larry must have understood. "Good boy."

And doing what I did—gaining my rhythm, watching in amazement as my dick moved between his pecs, my foreskin helping to make the action glide more easily, revealing my bright red knob glistening with my arousal before being covered again, over and over as I thrust and thrust—was something I'd also never experienced before.

I felt…special.

Why? 'Cause for a bottom boy like me, being able to fuck his man, even if a pec fuck, was something that meant more than just doing our thing, our designated roles as it were. It meant he respected me enough to let me do so.

He wanted me to spread my wings like our boundless love.

It didn't take long for me to climb towards the heights of my delight. I first felt it in the pit of my stomach as I rocked back and forth while on top of him. I even squeezed his pecs harder so they enveloped my dick even more, the perfect amount of pressure so I was masturbated by his muscles.

What a rush.

I sweated even more, began foaming at the mouth, I'm sure. I gasped and panted too. What a rush! Being a top sure was different, even if what I did didn't truly make me one.

As far as I was concerned, I was fucking my man! Giving him what he wanted. And wasn't that what love was all about?

Before too long, the fire in my stomach spread. I began quivering, arching my back, groaning from deep within my throat. I was close. So close. Too close.

"Cum for me, Jake-y!" Larry said trembling with as much excitement as me.

I didn't need to be told twice.

I came.

And man, did I come!

To see thick white ribbons of my excitement splatter all over his chin, mouth, nose, and cheeks was also something special, no mistake. It was awesome too. And jeez, I'd produced a hell of a lot of it again.

Two big loads in one night. Wow! I was a horny little devil all because of him, wasn't I? That time, and after I'd ejaculated, my balls achingly tight, all of me still quivering, I collapsed onto him as he'd done earlier onto me. I understood why. Cumming after fucking sure was a drain, wonderfully so, all that thrusting the reason. I sweated even more, dripping onto him.

"You look even sexier with my cum all over your face— real pretty."

Larry smiled. "You look sexy, period."

I quickly began licking the reward of my efforts off his face, eager and loving it. I tasted even saltier, my second ejaculation thicker as well. Tangier too. Still, I loved it. I could tell Larry did as well when we kissed, his moans matching mine.

After that, I licked his rock-hard abs clean of what'd dribbled out of me, as I'd promised. Although, lube-flavored jizz, that sort of oily taste added into the tangy saltiness, was something different to experience, no doubt. Still, our resulting kisses were awesome, as always. So much was going on I swear I got all emotional.

We were really into each other.

Something made more real when Larry, while caressing my back with his thick, beautiful fingers, said, "I love ya, Jake-y."

My heart stopped. "I love you too." And those words were never a truer thing spoken by me. Ever.

He chuckled, beaming a warm smile. "Ya complete me. Honest."

"Hard same."

Okay, that's when I did get all misty-eyed again. I held him. I was wrapped in his arms. I felt safe and protected, loved beyond measure at the same time.

After more snuggling and heaps of kisses, we eventually showered together. Yeah, gotta say, there were a couple of mutual but very hot blowjobs in the luxurious and glitzy bathroom after that. I'd never been blown surrounded by such extravagance, gold taps and all. Really fancy, for sure.

We then got into the tub, bubbles everywhere.

Suffice it to say, Larry bent me over the side and fucked me like I was his good and dirty boy again. I pec-fucked him after he gave me all of his love deep inside me.

What a night!

I'd be as sore as all hell in the morning, but loving the fact that I would be. Like I said, it was my reminder of how much we loved each other. What we did more and more that cemented our bond. Our special understanding of what we meant to each other as well.

When finally settled in for the night, me using Larry as my warm pillow, he embraced me, bringing me closer to him. I could hear his heartbeat, loud and strong. Mine still fluttered.

He said, "I forget to tell ya earlier, but did ya notice that guy lookin' at ya at *Badda-Bings?* The weaselly lookin' dude?"

I snorted a little laugh; I always got the attention of other men, attention I ignored. "Larry, a S.W.A.T. team with dogs and the bomb squad in tow could have raided my dad's place and I wouldn't have noticed—I only have eyes for you."

I ran my hands gently over his pecs and nipples to reinforce my words. My truth.

He sucked in a breath, worry crossing his big brow for a moment, which, in turn, worried me. "Well, the guy was actin' all suspicious, and I meant to follow it up but I got involved in other things, ya know."

Now I laughed. "Yeah, you got all involved inside my ass."

"And the rest of ya."

"That too."

He sat up. "But I'm bein' serious here, Jake-y. I think I recognized him in the brief moment I saw him, that guy. The weasel."

Now I was even more concerned. I sat up as well, looking him in the eyes. "What do you mean?"

He pondered for a moment before replying, "Do ya remember that crook we helped Hank arrest? I think it was when ya first came to work for me. That dirty no-good-for-nothin' drug dealer boss…the one with the nose. What was his name?" He shrugged. "Anyway, I think that the guy lookin' at ya all suspicious like was one of the men in his gang."

I was at a loss. "Err, that doesn't help me much. 'Cause FYI, everyone has a nose."

Larry laughed, his concern melting away for a moment. "Ya incorrigible, ya know that? No. He had a *huge* bulbous nose, all covered in acne or some shit. So red it was too. I looked it up one time to see what condition he had—rhinophyma was it, I think."

He had a good memory for weird facts but not names, it seemed. But for me, his description made something click. Lit a light, as it were.

"Oh yeah. I remember him."

"Yeah, too right. And if I'm gettin' that vibe I got off that weasel right, the one who disappeared 'fore I could say anythin', I reckon we'd better be careful."

Now I was really worried. "What are you saying, Larry?"

He looked puzzled, deep in thought too. "Nothin'. I dunno. A gut feelin' maybe. Maybe it's nothin'. But we'd better be on the lookout. Be careful. That's all I'm sayin'."

"I'm glad I've got you, then."

"I'm glad I've got ya too." He leant over, kissing me tenderly. "Now g'nite, beautiful." He held me with as much intention as always. I held him back, more so after what he'd said. "I gotta say, can't wait for us to wake up together."

"Hard hell yeah to that—and how would you like to be woken up, my handsome bara man?"

He blushed. "Your mouth around my cock would be a nice start."

"Done," I said, kissing him back. "And how about I get my ass around it after that?"

"I wouldn't want it any other way."

Sunday, July 25th

The next morning, light streaming in through the gap in the curtains, the day bright already despite the time of year, I woke with Larry's thick, muscular arms around me. I loved how I'd been comforted by him even when I dreamt.

Without hesitation I moved down on him, giving him what he desired. What I did as well. Of course, he pretended to remain asleep while I smelt, licked, kissed, and worshiped his morning glory with my salivating tongue and eager mouth, soon taking him in as deeply as I could, enjoying his taste, strong and pungent.

It turned me on.

So much so, as I sucked, slurped, and dribbled all over his throbbing length, breathless from my efforts, gulping, moaning, I rubbed myself against the sheets, already getting that wonderful feeling within me that could only mean one thing.

My fires had been ignited.

With more writhing while I blew my man, my hard-on pressed between me and the bed, my foreskin rubbing back and forth over my swollen knob to excite me even more, making me quiver in delight, I was ready to cum. Ready to let go simply 'cause of what I did to Larry.

What I did for him 'cause I wanted to do so without any thought of it being reciprocated either. 'Cause yeah, sometimes loving someone wasn't always about what could be taken, but what could be given as well.

And I would give myself to him, always.

Do anything for him.

'Cause I knew without a shadow of doubt he'd do the same for me. Without question. Without condition. We were one. And our togetherness made us stronger, our two souls intertwined for eternity.

That was love.

Our love.

Soon, Larry began breathing harder, squirming delightfully too. He clearly wasn't far behind me.

I was right.

He 'woke' when I'd clearly made him reach the point of no return. With shudders and groans, doing that cute face thing I loved, he quickly shot his load down my throat in thick, chunky wads.

I gulped it all down.

It was an awesome feeling to swallow all of what Larry gave me. 'Cause yeah, I'd also released at the same time, unable to help myself. Once I finished, the swirl of my ecstasy still coursing through me, that's when I realized it was true what they said around Dad's club about bottom boys always lying in the wet patch; whether their own they'd squirted out or from their man's leaking outta them, it didn't matter. Facts were facts.

I understood that all too well now.

Sweating, contented, and wonderfully breathless, I said, "You came a lot." My hardness ached 'cause I didn't soften, despite cumming.

"I was dreamin' of ya all night, that's why."

I kissed him; let him taste himself off my lips. "I made a big mess on the sheets."

He chuckled, holding me closer. "I don't think that'll be the worst thing house cleaning hasta deal with today—don't worry 'bout it."

I didn't worry. With the both of us in each other's arms, what was there to worry about, anyway? Not a goddamned thing.

Well, okay…maybe there was one thing to worry about, 'cause I realized something else. "I'm hungry." And then, of course, my stomach rumbled to emphasize my sudden need.

More light laughter from my man. "Didn't ya get enough meat and sauce just then?"

"Ha, ha, very funny." I tickled him. He wasn't very ticklish. Still, I enjoyed doing it 'cause it meant more moments where we were naked together before getting on with our day.

I wanted these intimate, carefree times to last forever.

Larry eventually ordered room service, expensive stuff cooked by a chef, no less. Still, no matter how it appeared on the menu, written in French to fancy it up even more, it amounted to eggs on toast with a side of crispy bacon. A glass of 'freshly squeezed' orange juice each too.

After eating, we showered.

Naturally, hot and steamy fucking resulted while we were in the bathroom. My god, I was going to leak his cum outta my ass for days, I knew it. I'd have to wear something to soak it all up. Did they make pads or whatever for bottom boys who'd gotten their fill after a night of unbridled passion with their man?

Probably not.

But as I contemplated my options, including douching to avoid any embarrassing stains on my clothing, I got distracted.

Distracted not by his attention and kisses—me also kissing him back in thanks for such an amazing night—but by his ringing phone. He parted our loving connection, frowning. His expression as disappointed as I felt.

"Gotta answer it, sorry. Business."

I nodded, my urges for him rising once more already. I didn't let him go. Couldn't. He was my life, my love, my very breath now.

Larry put his phone on speaker.

Senior Sergeant Hank Riley, our cop friend and the one Larry and I often worked with on cases, was on the other end. To me he sounded worried.

"Hey, Larry—you too, Jake. How are you both this morning?" he asked, his voice uneven. Before we could answer properly, he hastily added, "I think you should know we picked up a guy last night who Michael caught snooping around the staff only areas of the club."

Larry immediately replied, "The weaselly lookin' one?"

A harrumph of agreement. "He does look kind of weaselly, now you've mentioned it, yeah."

"I knew he was as suspicious as fuck," Larry confided. "What'd he say after ya arrested him?"

"Not much. They never do—not even when they lawyer up..."

A moment of pause, one that worried me. Something big was about to be dropped on us. I could feel it. Feel the uneasiness. The tension.

I gulped, and not in a good way.

Larry put his arm around me.

Hank continued, "Anyway. What he did enjoy telling us was that the man we incarcerated thanks to the information you two got off the streets…there's now a contract out on you, Jake."

I almost swallowed my tongue, my insides twisting as my blood turned to ice. The fancy hotel room around me spun and spun. I wobbled. Thank God I was holding onto Larry.

Or was he holding onto me?

Either way, I needed him, now more than ever.

Suffice it to say, it took me a moment to recover. Or was it longer? In any case, I was lying on the bed, Larry dabbing my forehead with a warm cloth, when I did come back to myself.

"A…a *contract*?" I mumbled; the words thick around my mouth, worry still stabbing at me like knives in my guts. "That means…that means they want me *dead*, doesn't it?"

Larry's eyes reflected more than concern. "Don't worry 'bout it—I'll protect ya with my life, Jake-y. *With my life.* That much I promise ya." He dropped the cloth to bring me into his arms; I felt his love through to my bones.

I appreciated what he did to try and comfort me.

Truly.

We kissed. Trembling kisses imbued with something I couldn't quantify, but to me it was something like sadness. That's how I interpreted it anyway, 'cause that's how I felt. An overwhelming sadness by what had transpired. I was a target.

I was also conflicted.

What could I do? What could Larry do? There had to be something we could do together about this...right? Perhaps Hank would help us. Wouldn't he? It was his job, after all.

I had to say, "I know you'll do your best, but you've never had a contract out on you before, have you?" I thought about that for a moment, deciding to reframe my question 'cause the first way I'd said it sounded so unlike me. Too demanding. And I didn't want to demand anything from Larry. "I mean, have you had a contract out on you before?"

He must have understood. His expression softened, softened like his big heart. "I haven't, no."

"Who...who did this? Do you remember his name?"

Something came over Larry; he clicked his fingers. "Mister Yaketsuku. Yeah, I remember him now, the one with the nose. That's the scum's name. The drug boss. Mister fucking Yaketsuku."

"What are we going to do?" I asked.

Larry climbed off me. "We go down to the station and find out what else the weasel can tell us, that's what we do, Jake-y."

"Will Hank let you do that?"

Larry winked. "I can be very persuasive."

"You mean you can get Judy to be very persuasive, don't you?"

Larry shrugged. "Same difference." He produced his phone...and yep, he called Judy.

I knew him so well already.

While he talked to Hank's 'girlfriend', I paced the room, my nerves and fears manifesting more and more simply 'cause I wasn't in control of what was going on. A weird feeling, for sure.

When the conversation finally ended, he took me by my hand. "Let's get our stuff packed up and get outta here."

"I take it Judy's going to help us."

Larry beamed a smile, showing all his pearly whites. "Like me, she'd do anythin' for ya. Heck, I reckon she'd even blow every bloke in Melbourne for ya, Jake-y."

I loved Judy, I really did. She was a good mate. "Would you do that for me?" I was being cheeky, finding my old self for a moment. A nice return...even if it was fleeting 'cause of my other worries vying for supremacy within me.

"Nope." Larry beamed a smile, squeezing my hand. "I won't touch no one else. Ya the only one for me, Jake-y. Now and forever."

I loved Larry even more. "And that's the right answer."

A couple of hours later, we were driving towards the station. The day had clouded over, ominous and black ahead of us. It would no doubt rain soon. Then again, maybe not. Melbourne's weather turned on a dime many times in a day.

"Are ya okay, Jake-y?"

I understood Larry asked to make conversation, 'cause I also knew he knew I wasn't all right. How could he not? For a start, I'd been quiet—so unlike me. I also hadn't stop fidgeting my right leg since we got into the car. Hadn't stopped staring out the window either.

And besides, even if I wasn't showing it, how would anyone be fine after hearing the news that a crime boss— even though in jail—had put a contract out on their life? It's not something that happened to normal folks, was it? All I wanted to do was love Larry; spend lazy days when we weren't working in his arms after his dick had been deep in me. I didn't want this.

Who would?

I returned my attention from the window to look at him. "I know I will be 'cause I have you. But yeah...my worry's still real, for sure."

While still concentrating on the road, eyes ahead, he replied, "I can pull over at a fast food place where I can blow ya in the toilet, if ya want me to. Get rid of some of that stress for ya."

I enjoyed so much how he thought of me, as his naughty boy who needed his love all the time. He was right though, not gonna lie. "To distract me, I'd rather suck on your dick right now."

"While I'm drivin'?"

"Why not?"

"Ahh...okay." Larry glanced at me, his cheeks all rosy. "How 'bout after I drive off from these next set of red lights, ya do just that?"

The car slowed as he approached the lights in question.

I smiled, my worries melting away for a moment. My stomach turned in that delightful way and I felt myself stir. Got really hard for him.

"Although, you do realize what I'll do to you will make me cum as well."

"I know—wouldn't want it any other way, would I?"

A thought struck me. "But I'll have to cum in my undies, 'cause I'm pretty sure you won't want my jizz all over your car's interior."

"Ya right, ya will." Larry winked. "But don't worry, Jake-y. I'll lick up ya boy juice outta ya jocks once we've parked. And 'sides, we have our cases from the hotel in the boot. Ya can change into a fresh pair 'fore we go see Hank."

I agreed.

Nothing more needed to be said.

With a lust-filled smile, I leant over so I could begin unzipping Larry's fly in preparation. As I did so, he braked, stopping the car at the red lights. I brushed my fingers over his bulge, noticing he was as hard as I was. It was such a good feeling knowing that what I do to him made him as horny as it did me. I reached into his pants, feeling his warm and throbbing dick moments later, grabbing it, squeezing it, and pulling back on his foreskin to get at his swollen head. I ran my fingertips over his knob, over his wettened slit from his excitement to tease him before my mouth did its thing.

Larry groaned his approval.

I licked my lips, getting myself ready. I missed the pungent, manly taste of him, even though I'd tasted it only a couple of hours ago in the hotel room. Still, I needed to experience it again already. I needed to worship him. Smell him. Suck on him. Make him cum. And experience it I would, for sure.

"Ready?" I asked.

"Yeah," he shuddered a breath, "I sure am!"

But before I could fish out his dick properly, able to go down on him without any obstacles, Larry jumped, startling me.

"What the hell?!" he exclaimed, grabbing my hand to stop me from proceeding.

I sat up, worry finding me. "What's wrong?"

He zipped up. "Shit! Someone's following us! That's what's wrong."

"What?" My heart found my throat as it beat worryingly fast to lodge itself in there.

I turned so I could look out the rear window. Sure enough, two black cars—sleek Mercedes they were, complete with blacked-out windows—went from going behind us to quickly pulling up beside us while we were stopped at the lights.

A heartbeat later, the doors of the two cars opened and many men poured out, surrounding us. I yelped, panicking now. Larry reached over towards the glove box. What was in there, I didn't know; hopefully, a gun to defend us.

Then, a loud bang.

Larry's window smashed in. My ears rang, and it took me a moment to even think. Everything was happening so fast.

Another bang, even louder.

Shattered glass covered me like broken diamonds

everywhere. My window had also been broken. That time, I didn't scream. I just went numb with fear. I couldn't believe this was happening. This sort of thing only happened in the movies…right? A cold sweat found me as my dread rose. I didn't know what to do. I couldn't move; I was that scared.

When I saw two men roughly grab my man, that's when I came to life, everything else pushed aside. "Larry!"

I tried to reach for him.

A split second later, Larry's seatbelt was unclipped, and he was yanked from the car, yelling his head off in protest. Sure, he laid in a few punches, some connecting to faces, but there were too many of them.

He was overpowered, dragged away from me.

"Larry!" I screamed and screamed, my heart bleeding for him, hope fading, as my spirits sank even more. What could I do? "Larry! *Larry!*"

Before I could do anything, call the cops, go after him or whatever, anything, I felt a strong hand clamp upon my shoulder. It hurt. I winced, turning to look into the cold, hard eyes of the man who'd shattered my window.

"Don't even think about doing anything heroic, boy," the man said smoothly, too calm for the chaos around me for my liking; I could hear Larry struggling, shouting, calling my name, as he was bundled into the boot of one of the Mercedes. "Or I'll put a bullet in your skull. Kill you dead. Got it?"

I gulped.

Something cold and hard was pressed against my temple. I didn't need to guess what it was. I knew. I was scared outta my mind now. That's when I felt my bladder release, the awful warmth that followed between my legs. My vision went misty as I became overwhelmed, as my emotions released with it. As I feared for Larry's life. My own too.

But I could only think of my big, handsome bara man. Through trembling lips, I barely managed, "Wh…what are…you going to d-do to Larry?"

The man smiled cruelly, one that looked like a scar across his wicked, sneering face. "I wouldn't worry your pretty little head about that. I'd worry more about what's going to happen to you, hey?"

From somewhere deep down, dredging it up to do so, I had to ask, "Wh…what are you g-going to do to me?"

That's when I heard the screeching of tyres as the Mercedes with Larry inside it sped off, the traffic lights turning green.

"I'm going to do this." And with that he raised his arm.

The butt of the gun must have struck me, because after the searing pain I felt that knocked the air from my lungs, there was nothing.

Only darkness.

Unknown Date

I woke with blurry vision, bright lights above making it worse, and aching all over. But jeez, did my head pound when I tried to move; saying I experienced a monster of a headache was like the understatement of the century, that's for sure.

A shadow came over me.

I blinked, trying to clear the fuzziness from my eyes. When I could see again, I realized it was my dad. His look of worry was nothing compared to how I felt at seeing him. The relief. It was also nothing compared to the feeling of loss I experienced now that Larry had been taken away from me. How I'd been unable to do anything about it but piss myself like a frightened little boy facing his schoolyard bullies.

So many mixed and terrible emotions.

Argh!

Before I could utter a word, in explanation or otherwise, a justification even, my dad held me, obviously happy I was conscious. It took a moment, but suffice it to say that's when I let everything go.

That's when I cried like a baby in his arms.

Dad held me forever.

When I'd wet his chest with my tears, my snot and mucus added, because I really was a mess, a complete disaster, missing Larry to my soul, to every atom in my body, Dad moved so he could look me in the eyes.

"I'm so glad you're okay, Jake." Dad's eyes were red and misty; seemed he got emotional too. "I don't know what I'd do if anything happened to you."

I took a moment to understand his words. And yeah, even though I was happy I hadn't been killed, unbelievably so, you have no idea, 'cause life meant hope, I had to ask, "Where am I, Dad?"

"You're in the hospital under observation—you took a nasty bump to the head. You've been here overnight."

I lifted my hand. I felt a bandage. "It was no accident what happened. The guy hit me with his gun, Dad. Hit me!"

"I know."

I wanted to find out one thing and one thing only. "What about Larry? Any word?"

Dad shook his head. "We don't know anything… sorry," Dad replied. That's when Tachibana came into view. Dad and his boyfriend held each other, looking at me, concern from the both of them.

"What?" I asked, feeling a sense of dread, more so.

That's when Hank approached. It sure was a crowd around me, wasn't it? He was in uniform too. No doubt he had something serious to say.

When he spoke…yeah, I was right. "I'm afraid it was all a setup, Jake," he said with a defeatist huff.

"What do you mean?" Fear stabbed at my heart once more—the bastard, it was.

I hated it.

Hank sucked in another breath. "By telling us there was a contract out on you, they knew Larry would act. They knew he would try and get to me as well."

I drained, going numb. "They…they were waiting for us to leave the hotel room?"

Hank nodded. "They were—Larry was their real target."

I asked, "How would they have known where we were?"

Dad chimed in, "It wasn't exactly a secret, was it?"

Tachibana contributed, "Like everyone else, Jake, they would have known about the both of you going to the hotel from the guy we caught snooping around the club."

My heart sank. "Yeah, you're right."

Hank offered a smile, even if it wasn't reassuring. Not really. "We're working on the scene of the crime at the moment. Perhaps that'll give us some clues."

Surprise found me. "You don't know who did this?"

I moved so I could sit up and immediately wished I hadn't. My head throbbed terribly even more. I winced too. Dad tried to steady me while Tachibana arranged the pillows behind me so I was supported. I felt more comfortable thanks to their attention. I smiled at them both, even if it was somewhat hollow 'cause I didn't have my man with me.

"It's not a matter of knowing who," Hank supplied, "but which gang is responsible."

Now I was confused. "Huh?" 'Cause surely the crime boss Larry and me helped lock up, Mister Yaketsuku his name, was responsible. Right?

Even Dad and Tachibana shared my expression.

Hank sat on the bed; it creaked under his weight. "What I mean by that is there are many dealers in the city. Too many gangs associated with them as well." He sighed. "And we know Mister Yaketsuku had his sticky fingers in many underworld pies, so we're not sure which gang he recruited to do his dirty work. Once we do know, rest assured, we'll then find Larry."

But there was something in his voice, his tone, his hesitancy too, that told me he wasn't telling me everything.

I wasn't deterred, though. "Then why don't you ask him? He's in jail, isn't he? Ask him where Larry is."

Hank nodded. "Yes, Mister Yaketsuku's in jail, but don't you think we've already tried that? He won't talk to us."

"Then what can we do?" My heart sank to my feet, I'm sure.

Dad held me again.

But Hank finally smiled; a nice sight. "Unofficially, of course, I can organize something…how shall we say?… something *unorthodox* to help us get the information we need."

All of us looked at the cop. "Um…what do you mean by that, Hank?" I questioned.

He winked. "Men in jail, especially those sentenced long term, want their desires met above all else. I so happen to know a certain someone who can provide such services."

"Judy!" we all said in unison.

Hank now beamed. "Yes, Judy. And she'll do whatever it takes to help all of us—you most of all, Jake."

Dad asked, "You don't…you know, mind that Judy's a sex worker who's helping you, Hank?"

"Not at all," he replied immediately, holding his smile. "Sex work is work, and Judy wants to help us—besides, she *can* suck a golf ball through a garden hose." He laughed lightly. "I should know. And most men can't resist that kind of action, even crooks. So it's all good, I say."

Hank surprised me even more. He really was an open-minded guy considering his profession. And I knew Judy escorted for herself in her spare time, Friday nights and weekends mostly. Everyone knew it, really. She only worked in Mister Anderson's office—where my old job as the gofer boy was before I began to get serious with Larry—to give her some extra stability.

I really did love her. Loved her to bits.

But Dad was a touch more pragmatic. "Err…what if this Mister Yaketsuku character prefers guys and not busty blonde women who can give great blowjobs, as you say?"

Hank snorted. "We'll soon find out, won't we?"

With a harrumph, determination coming over me too, I said, "If it turns out that way, I'll blow the bastard until I've drained his balls dry if it means getting my Larry back to me."

It was now my turn to be looked at with shock, Dad's eyes the widest.

Before Dad could protest or otherwise Hank raised his hand. "Now hang on, let's not be hasty. If it turns out Mister Yaketsuku bats for the same team he's on, and that's a big if, I wouldn't put you in such danger, Jake. Not a chance in hell."

"But…"

Hank continued, "We have other people for that sort of thing; trained professionals who can handle such tasks—all on the down low and off the record, naturally."

I then had a thought, one of concern for my friend. "Has Judy been trained to handle such things?" 'Cause yeah, I had to admit, I worried about her.

"She has been, yes," Hank proclaimed proudly. "Did it myself."

Dad and Tachibana looked at each other.

I suppressed a giggle as best I could, only smirking in the end. I had a fair idea of the training Hank gave Judy… or, more likely, it was the other way around. Yeah, no doubt about that, Judy was the boss.

There was no argument from any of us after that. Seemed everything was set—even if it wasn't exactly standard police procedure. Hank sure liked to color outside the boxes, didn't he?

Good on him.

The only thing I worried about now was how Larry was fairing. Was he okay? Had he been injured during his abduction? Or even afterwards? Was he being looked after if he had been?

Jeez, I missed him so much it hurt me to my bones. To my soul. My very being. I needed him. Needed him more than anything else.

And yes, I would do anything to get him back. *Anything!*

But worst of all, 'cause I couldn't help thinking such things, despite not wanting to, was the worst-case scenario.

Was my man even alive?

That thought almost made me faint and my head hurt even more. I became overwhelmed again. Dad held me tightly. I fell into his arms, bringing my head close to his chest again, my only comfort right now.

I cried.

I cried until I couldn't cry anymore.

Tuesday, July 27th

I was discharged from the hospital in the morning after the doctors did their rounds and agreed my injury wouldn't cause me too much bother. I didn't have a concussion. Bonus!

Dad and Tachibana were with me, fussing over me. I really appreciated their support and care during my darkest days. My heart ached even more for Larry with each passing moment, though.

Dad drove me home.

I lived with him and Tachibana since I'd come out, after telling the world I wanted to be with Larry, that I loved him. My mum didn't want anything to do with me after that, me being one of those "disgusting homosexuals who corrupted all the good of this world" as she put it—as she screamed it at me, really. I didn't bother arguing with her. It wasn't worth it. I would have thought her love for me before I came out could have changed her attitude.

It didn't.

Made it worse, really.

How could someone hate their son so much 'cause of who they wanted to be with? Who they loved? I didn't get it. Nope. Never will either, I supposed.

As I sat down…no, as I flopped down onto the nearest couch, Dad handing me a cup of coffee, smelling great, all aromatic, my phone rang. I didn't get a sip of it before I was disturbed.

I put it on speaker.

"Where are you, Jake?" Hank asked without asking how I was, which meant that what he wanted to say must be important.

"I just got home. Why?"

"Can we meet? Not at the station. Somewhere else?"

"Um…alright." Now I was curious. "Where?"

This all sounded rather cloak and dagger, didn't it? I would have thought Hank wanted to meet at the station. Then again, I remembered that our little covert plan I affectionately called 'operation Judy' wasn't exactly standard procedure, was it? I'd even venture to say Hank was acting independently 'cause it was Larry—his best friend—involved in all this.

"How about the coffee shop on Collins Street?"

Dad interjected, "The Veranda Café?"

"That's the—" Hank's voice halted. Another voice was heard in the background, even though I didn't hear what was spoken between them. He clearly had his hand over the phone's speaker to talk privately with the other person.

When he did speak to us again, he only said, "See you there in an hour," and hung up.

I looked at Dad.

He shrugged, taking the cup of coffee from me. "Looks like we're going out to get coffee."

"I guess so."

At that moment, Tachibana entered from the kitchen.

He was carrying a plate full of Tim Tam biscuits and finger-sized slices of chocolate cake arranged neatly onto it.

Dad stood, taking the plate off his boyfriend with one hand, still holding my cup of coffee in the other. "It looks like we're going out for morning tea and coffee, babe. Sorry."

Tachibana's eyebrows rose. "We've only just got home from the hospital." He glanced between his plate of prepared treats and my steaming hot coffee, freshly brewed. "What's the rush?"

"Hank called," I said, as if that would explain it.

Clearly it must have, 'cause Tachibana nodded. "I'll go get the car keys."

The Veranda Café wasn't busy.

A good thing too. Not 'cause anyone would have known about what we were doing there, other than the obvious 'we're getting coffee' of course, but 'cause I kind of felt weird that we were meeting like this. It felt dishonest. And no, even if it was with Hank, I didn't feel any better about it. Then again, the cop would no doubt give me some news about Larry.

My Larry.

That was worth anything and any risk, truly.

Hank arrived ten minutes after we'd ordered. The coffee was nowhere near as good as Dad's. The coffee I missed out on. The cake accompanying it wasn't as good as what Tachibana made either.

"Hey, all," Hank said casually as he sat down, but I

could tell he was worried; a neck vein bulged, and he glanced from side to side.

"What's happened?" I asked, not bothering to stand on any ceremony. Why should I? We all knew why this meeting was happening and what it was about, didn't we?

Dad reiterated, "Tell us any news, no matter how good or bad, Hank."

Tachibana nodded, sipping his drink—a hot chocolate.

Hank replied, "To cut to the chase, as I'm sure you're keen for me to do, Judy didn't get too much out of Mister Yaketsuku other than a name."

"What name?" we all said together.

"Fingers," was Hank's rather enigmatic reply.

"That's a name?" I was taken aback. "You're kidding me, right?"

Hank nodded. "Unfortunately, I'm not kidding, no."

But Dad said, "You mean 'Fingers' as in Fingers McGee, right?"

Hank sighed, again looking from side to side. "The very same."

"Shit." Dad didn't look happy now.

I had to ask, "Who's Fingers McGee and what's he got to do with this?"

Hank and Dad shared worried glances. Tachibana simply looked as I did; not a bloody clue as to what this was all about. Who this 'Fingers' bloke was either.

It was Dad who finally spoke. "From what I've heard around the club, Fingers is a sort of…specialist."

"What do you mean?" But my fears were growing; I didn't like where the road of the conversation was taking me—straight into a deep, dark forest full of monsters, no doubt.

"If it's true that Fingers is involved, it means two things," Hank began.

"What are they?" I asked before letting him continue.

"Please, I'm getting to that, Jake." Hank cleared his throat. "It means that Larry's alive, but—"

"That's good!" I almost stood up, wanting to shout my joy that Larry would be back with me soon…hopefully.

Dad put his hand gently upon my shoulder. "Fingers is notorious for his…unusual use of certain medical instruments. He was once a surgeon, but now…" a swallow from Dad, "I'm afraid to tell you this, Jake, because it sickens me to my stomach, but it also means Larry is no doubt being…tortured."

His words hit me like a tonne of bricks. I went all emotional. Overcome. Everything spun around me. Worse than that, I wanted to cry and hit something all in one instant.

Someone was going to pay for this.

While Dad held me, my support, my comfort, wonderfully so 'cause I had no one else, and certainly not my Larry, I mumbled, "We've g-got to find him as s-soon…as soon as w-we can. We've got to!"

"We will," Hank said, surprisingly reassuringly.

I looked up, straight into his eyes to gauge the truth of his words. There was no lie there. None I could tell, anyway.

Tachibana chimed in, "How can you be so sure, Officer Hank?"

"Please, you don't have to be so formal, Tachibana. Just call me Hank, okay?"

Tachibana nodded. "Hank it is, then."

"But to answer your question, Jake, I'm sure because if I know crooks like I do, *and I know them well*, it seems to me the gang Mister Yaketsuku recruited is trying to gain territory."

I still didn't understand. "What's all that got to do with Larry?" I asked, still a wrecked mess from the last bomb dropped.

Hank rubbed his thick chin. "They've got Fingers involved for two reasons."

Dad clicked his fingers. "One of them being to get information out of Larry about any rival gangs' movements and the like, correct?"

"Correct!" Hank agreed, pointing at him, smiling.

"What's the other one?" Tachibana asked, beating me to it.

Dad replied, "You already know that one."

Again, my confusion reigned. "I do?" I had to think for a moment. Recall events. Then it clicked. "Oh, yeah. Revenge. Revenge for what me and him did to help you put Mister Yaketsuku behind bars. Am I right?"

Hank nodded, now pointing at me. "Yep, you are."

I'd finally got something. Wonders will never cease.

Dad said, "What do you plan to do?"

"We fight fire with fire," Hank replied with determination coming over him.

We all looked at each other, Hank most of all.

Yeah, my spark of understanding didn't last long. I'd

caught the first available bus straight into the land of confusion again, I had.

As such, I found myself saying, "I hate repeating myself here, but how does that work?"

Hank shifted his weight. "I don't think we have any choice but to ask Joe for help. Not now. Not seeing as we know Fingers is involved."

Reading between the lines there, I imagined Larry didn't have much time. Which scared the bejesus outta me, to be honest. My stomach turned. Terribly so. I couldn't even imagine what my big handsome bara man was going through.

I had to stop myself from crying again.

But something else then clambered to the forefront of my thoughts. I blinked. I realized this was getting ridiculous. I was really a fish out of water, wasn't I?

'Cause yeah, who the fuck was Joe?

Hank must have caught my expression of bewilderment, written plain on my face along with the rest of my fears, no doubt. "Joe's a…*special* kind of guy. Truly," he began. "And I've got to admire him in a way, because he's such a smooth talker, a real pro, I reckon he could get into the Vatican dressed as a Satanic cult leader. He's that good. He's therefore the perfect person to use to find out where Larry is."

"Why didn't we just ask him for help first, then?" I asked.

Dad, his hand still upon me, said, "The word is Joe's the sort of guy everyone instantly trusts. And when he is trusted, that's when his true nature is revealed. Apparently, not many gay men can resist him…until it's too late, that is."

"He doesn't sound too bad," Tachibana chimed in.

"Joe's a murderer and rapist," Hank explained. "And he does it in that order. He's a necrophiliac." I didn't know what a necrophiliac was as such, but from the context of what Hank had said it didn't take much of a guess, did it? I shuddered at the thought. How many men had he…killed and then…eww? Was that even a thing? It had to be if there was a word for it.

I shuddered again, my skin crawling that time.

Hank continued, "And just so you know, Joe's only out of jail because he's agreed to work with the police, be on his best behavior too. It's an opportunity I can't pass up on, even if what I'm doing is off the record, so to speak. And besides, the advantage that we have here is that most don't even know he's out of there yet. That's why he's the perfect man for the job."

"When can we ask this…this Joe person to help us?" I asked, hopes rising within me despite my disgust.

"I can ask him as soon as *you* want me to, Jake."

I then felt prickling heat at the back of my neck. "Um…why do you need my permission?"

Dad immediately said, "I know what you're thinking, Hank, and that's a hard hell no. A *hard* hell no!"

Tachibana agreed.

I was still clueless…for a moment. That was until the pieces fit into place. Through trembling lips, my stomach flipping, feeling sick, I said, "You're asking me 'cause I'm the sweetener for the deal you're going to make with Joe, aren't I?"

Hank nodded slowly, forlornly too. "Joe likes young men. So yes, as soon as he sees you, Jake, he'll agree to whatever we want from him. But it'll have to be you who asks him for help. He won't accept anyone else; I already know that."

Tachibana cleared his throat. "I can do it—I'm young enough."

"You're over twenty-one." Hank shook his head. "Jake's only eighteen."

"That's unacceptable," Dad blurted, cheeks reddening. "I won't have my son put in any more danger. He's been through enough already." He was angry...or getting that way fast.

Tachibana now comforted him.

But before Dad could say anything more, cause me any doubt about what had panned out and where I found myself, between a rock and a hard place, really, I interjected, "I'll do it." And that was the truth. I'd do whatever it took to get my Larry back.

Including asking a necrophiliac for help, one who'd probably want to kill me then fuck me. And yeah, that thought wasn't one I'd ever believe I'd have swimming around in my head along with all my other worries lately, that's for sure.

Wednesday, July 28th

Things weren't so good the next day. I hadn't slept. I tossed and turned all night, worrying about Larry. What they were doing to him. What that Fingers character was doing to him, more to the point. I hadn't eaten much either. Not even when Dad made his speciality for breakfast, an omelette he referred to as his 'gay surprise' 'cause he put spicy sausages in it. I just picked at it, pushing the rest around the plate with my fork.

"Please eat up, Jake—you'll need your energy for today," Tachibana said, always polite.

"Why?" I snorted. "So I'll have the energy to fend off a known necrophiliac who'll want to pound my dead ass until he gets off?" I really didn't mean that to sound so harsh.

Tachibana's eyebrows rose, but he didn't say anything more other than look at Dad, worry drawn on his brow.

"It's alright." Dad put his arms around me. "Larry will be back with you soon, I know it."

I knew he was trying to be optimistic. I appreciated it. But how could he be so sure? How could anyone? But with him holding me, and my thoughts spiralling again, that's when I became overwhelmed and began crying big heaving tears. I missed Larry so much!

And yeah, I'd cried so much lately it was ridiculous. Truly. Jeez, I was such a soft boy, wasn't I? Still, if I wasn't,

Larry wouldn't have fallen in love with me. So, there was that, right? Come to think of it, I actually liked how I was in touch with my emotions, even if they ran away with me most times, like right now.

Dad let me do my thing.

I moved so he could hold me proper. Be my comfort. My support. He was so patient I couldn't help love him even more, even if our relationship hadn't exactly started out well. Before I came out, before I realized that he was on my side, always had been, I was a jerk to him. I hated admitting that now.

I wasn't a jerk anymore.

I loved my dad to pieces. Loved his boyfriend Tachibana too.

When I'd composed myself enough, wiping my eyes, still affected by my outburst though, I ate as much as I could of the breakfast he'd cooked, even if it took ages. It was the least I could do for him seeing as he made it specially for me.

By the time Tachibana began clearing away the dishes, the doorbell rang to make my heart leap into my throat. This was it. The moment I'd been dreading. The moment I wanted to get over and done with as soon as possible. Quicker than that.

It'd been arranged that Hank would bring the Joe character to us. 'Cause yeah, due to the nature of his 'off the record' operation, one Hank assured us he had the approval of his boss, but I wasn't so sure, it couldn't be done at the station.

Hank also assured us, especially me, mostly me actually,

that all safety precautions would be adhered to. What that meant I had no bloody idea. Would Hank arrive with the necrophiliac in a straitjacket?

"This is it!" Dad went to the door. "Show time!"

I heard a discussion.

Moments later, and I have to admit, one of the most handsome men I'd ever seen, handcuffed and led by Hank, was brought into the front lounge room where I now waited, nervous, leg twitching, sweating really.

Joe was stunning.

I could see why gay guys would be all over him like a rash…to their demise, I might add. Not only was he all lovely blond hair, long at the front and flicked back just so, he had soft features, great lips and chin, and was tall but not too thin or too big. He was everything. A sort of Swiss army knife of what appealed to gays, really.

What's more, his face brightened as soon as he must have seen me, letting me believe I was the only one in the room who had his attention. Which yeah, that was true too.

I swallowed, hard.

Joe said, "My, my, Hank. When I agreed to this meeting, you didn't tell me I'd be in the presence of someone so delectable, did you?"

And that's when my skin crawled.

Not because of what Joe said, his voice as smooth as silk sheets over intertwined lovers, but the way he said it. Like I was his next victim. Well, that's how I felt…with good reason.

"I'm Jake," I said nervously, not bothering to stand or add that I was pleased to meet him.

I really wasn't pleased to meet him. And I only agreed to this meeting 'cause it would help me get Larry back. Otherwise, there'd be no chance in hell I'd be sitting in the same room as this sick creep.

Hank sat Joe in an opposite chair, the farthest away from me. He didn't remove the cuffs. Good. But that's when I realized my heart was racing.

Dad and Tachibana sat either side of me, protecting me, no doubt.

Hank, clearing his throat, shifting his weight as he stood over Joe, said, "Jake here wants to ask you for help, Joe."

Joe smiled, one that filled the room it was so lovely. But I knew the reason behind it. The darkness it held. "Well then, let Jake ask me for it."

I gulped again.

Hank looked at me. Dad shuffled closer.

I said, "Umm…err…Joe, I'd like to ask you for help, as Hank said. So yeah…here it is. Me asking."

Joe held his smile, one that would be like a flame to all those gay moths, I'm sure. "And what will you do for me if I do help you, Jake?"

"Now hang on, Joe," Hank interjected. "We discussed this and there's no way—"

Joe shot Hank a dirty look, the first time his calm façade cracked. "Let Jake speak. I want to know how much his man means to him if he's willing to ask me for help." The cracks then repaired themselves. That was quick. Joe added, "What will *you* do for *me*, Jake?"

"I…I don't know," I admitted, 'cause I didn't. "What

do you want from me, Joe? I need my Larry back…and I'd do whatever it'll take for that to happen. Honest as I sit here."

Dad sucked in a breath. I knew from that I hadn't exactly gone to plan. I was the one supposed to be in control here.

Joe, however, laughed. "Oh, honey. You can't give me what I want—and I don't want any more jail time as a result of it." He moved to get up. "It seems there's nothing more to discuss, is there?"

Yeah, I knew what that was. What he wanted. But there was no chance in hell I'd drop dead so that he could fuck my cold, dead corpse. No chance.

Although despite the shutdown, I realized I was desperate. As such, terrible nerves found me as I realized one thing.

Joe wanted me to beg.

"Then *please*, w-what can I…give you?" I became jittery and had to compose myself before my emotions got the better of me again. I didn't want a scene. Not here. Not now. "There must be s-something I can do to convince you to help me, Joe. Please…*please* help me!"

Joe sat back down proper, smiling again. "Hmm, you are delicious, Jake. That's not in doubt. But yes, you're right. There may be one thing you can do for me. If everyone here agrees, of course."

A movement either side of me as Dad and Tachibana shifted their weight now, the couch's leather creaking, loud within the fresh silence of the room. It was like waiting for a viper to strike, it really was. The tension was unbelievable.

My heart pounded even more. Jeez, sweat dripped down my back too.

Hank was the only one who seemed composed.

I whispered, "Then tell me…tell me what I can do for you."

"You can touch yourself for me." He sat forward, handcuffs clinking as he rubbed himself between his legs, moaning. "I also want you to cum into your underwear, your best pair, then give it to me as a souvenir of our little agreement. That way I can smell your desperation and need to get your Larry back whenever I want. How does that sound, Jake? Can you do that for me?"

Without delay, giving him no reason to doubt me, I replied, "I'll do it."

"I need to watch you too. Otherwise, it's no deal. Understand?"

I nodded. "Sure…whatever." 'Cause all things considered, me giving the perverted creep my cum-stained undies wasn't the worst thing I'd imagined would have happened, that's for sure.

"And I do believe that you'd better get on with it as soon as possible," Joe added lasciviously. "If what I hear is correct about Fingers being involved, your Larry won't have much time."

"He won't?" My heart almost exploded within my throat at that.

I gasped.

Dad and Tachibana did too.

Joe calmly shook his head. "Not many can…how shall

we say?...last too long under Fingers' special kind of attention."

Something then struck me, the way Joe sounded so confident. Full of himself too. He knew a lot more than he was letting on, I could feel it to my bones.

As such, and with a terrible realisation dawning on me, I had to ask, "You…you already know where Larry is, don't you?"

His smile went even more carnal. "Masturbate for me, Jake. Then give me what I want from you, and you'll have your answer. That much I guarantee."

I was wide-eyed and unbelieving. "Fine. Where do you want to do this, then? 'Cause I want to get it over and done with, that's for sure."

I was asking Hank more than anyone 'cause here and now was a good a place and time as any. In fact, that's when I realized I was already moving so I could unbutton my jeans. I didn't care if Dad or Tachibana watched me stroke my dick for Larry's sake. I didn't care about anything. I only wanted my man to be back with me where he belonged.

I needed Larry.

And if that meant cumming in front of my family, a cop too, for a sick criminal like Joe who had the information I needed, then so be it. I was ready.

Really ready.

But that's when Hank finally spoke. "Hang on, Jake. I think we've got to be careful here. Don't you?"

Dad also came to life. "And what's more, how the hell can we trust *him*? How do we know that he'll even help us once he's got what he wants from my son? Got his little 'souvenir' from him, as it were?"

Joe shrugged. "You can't, can you?" His oily smile remained. "And that's the beauty of all this, isn't it?"

I hated the man.

Hank growled. "Don't take advantage of the situation, Joe, or I'll—"

"Or you'll do what exactly, Hank?" Joe shot back. "Tell your superior about this little side project of yours? How you involved me? That you're also agreeing to my unconventional demands by letting an innocent eighteen-year-old lad jerk himself off all because you want me to tell you where your friend is being held by Mister Yaketsuku's newest boys?"

"Ah, so you *do* know where Larry is." Hank's lips pressed together, a small smirk of victory, no doubt. "Thanks for that."

Joe sucked in a breath, composing himself quickly though. "Oh, well played, Hank. Well played, I say."

"I learnt from the best."

Joe nodded. "Alright. I do know where Larry is, that's the truth. But I've decided to raise the stakes now that we're at our end game, so to speak." He pointed to me with his handcuffed hands. "Your little bottom boy there has to suck me off as well as cum onto his underwear. He's also got to swallow what I give him too. That's the deal now. Take it or leave it. No skin off my sack if you don't."

Dad and Tachibana screamed their protest, deafening me.

Before I could respond, tell them that it was my

decision 'cause it involved Larry and me, and not them, Hank raised his hand.

The room quietened.

He ordered, "Jake, get into your room and do what you've got to do. We'll see you soon."

Joe shot Hank a glare that could kill. "That's not the deal, copper."

In return, Hank laughed, right in Joe's face. "I don't answer to you, *Joe*. Something you've clearly forgotten."

Joe's calm expression was shattered, that time not recovering so quickly. Not recovering at all.

Dad breathed a sigh of relief. As did I, to be honest.

Hank undeterred, continued, "You'd better pray I don't alter the deal any further. As it stands, you'll accept Jake's gift without protest. When you do, you'll then tell us where Larry is or I'll have your ass hauled back into jail so fast your head'll spin. Got it?"

Joe's face then went beetroot red, but his shoulders slumped; all his confidence of before completely dissipating. "Hmph…make sure you cum a lot then, boy," he said, defeated.

"Um…okay," I offered, standing, unsure what'd happened.

Dad and Tachibana patted me on my back, like I was about to enter a boxing ring or something as the favorite.

I felt so weird.

Then again, what other word could describe what'd transpired?

None.

As I made my way to my room, I heard Joe say, "Oh,

and I don't want any cheap old pair jizzed into either. Only your best, boy. Got it?"

"You'll get what you get, Joe," Hank replied. "Be grateful for it." Although I had the feeling Hank, my dad, and Tachibana were happy about how things had turned out considering what *could* have happened.

I was happy too, being honest.

Yes, I would do anything for Larry; also realising I wouldn't cheat on him. No way. Not ever. Not even to save his life. And what I meant by that was I knew to my soul, 'cause yeah, with my family and Hank and all my other friends behind me, backing me up, it'd never come to that, anyway.

Just like it didn't now. And there was no use worrying or even thinking about something that'd never happen. Right?

I walked down the hallway.

More words were spoken between Hank and Joe, between all of them, but I didn't hear any of it. The drama of what had happened prickling freshly at the back of my neck, the realisation that I'd soon know where Larry was, hope rekindling, made my head spin.

I felt giddy.

Although I did have another thought, one more worrying as I entered my bedroom. How the fucking hell was I supposed to get a hard-on after all that craziness? 'Cause despite my bravado and determination earlier, now that it'd come down to it, I certainly wasn't in the mood to jerk off. Not until my man was with me again, that's for sure. I sighed. It seemed to me that I had no choice right now. I'd have to try and ejaculate while soft, then.

Yeah, that's what I'd have to do.

I touched myself, rubbing my groin, desperate and getting more so.

Nothing.

No movement whatsoever.

Could a guy even do it while remaining flaccid? I mean, I'm sure it was possible, but even so, I bet it wouldn't produce much cum. Hardly any, I'd imagine.

Maybe it would have been better if Joe was watching me. Might spur me on, get me worked up a bit, at least. Perhaps. Then again, I shuddered at that thought. I didn't want him looking at me, not even with my clothes on.

This was indeed something I had to do alone.

While attempting to arouse myself, still nothing, I stared at my chest of drawers for ages, trying to think of anything in there that'd get me excited enough to do what was expected of me.

Maybe I could use my dildo.

I shook that idea from my thoughts. Using it would take too long. I wanted this over and done with quickly. Too bad I didn't have any of that 'realistic jizz' lube stashed away I knew you could buy online. I'd then just squirt a pair of undies with that and be done with it.

Too bad.

But my attention was now on what pair I could use to do the deed onto. I had many pairs. Too many. What guy didn't? Actually, scratch that. What *gay* guy didn't—I couldn't speak for the straights. Underwear was like our brand, it really was.

I pulled out a pair of *Aussie Bums*, my cutest ones with the lifting pouch and double vents at the front, so sexy. They were bright red, complete with a thick white band across the top emblazoned with the brand.

That should do it—they weren't my most expensive pair, Joe wasn't getting those, but they weren't cheap either. A happy medium, I believed.

As soon as I retrieved the pair, I sniffed them, me being into that sort of thing. I sighed. They were freshly washed, of course. Only the scent of the laundry detergent Dad used could be detected, all florally and not arousing at all. Then again, they wouldn't be in my drawers if they weren't clean, would they? So no, nothing to get me stirred up there.

Nope.

Not a chance.

Okay, maybe if I rubbed myself with them. That could work, right? I undid my pants and pulled down the undies I was wearing. Now exposed, I looked down at my unhappy little man. I had no choice but to get to work, even if my body didn't want to cooperate.

I climbed onto my bed after removing all of my clothing, socks too. If I rubbed my own odors off onto the pair of undies that I was going to gift Joe, then perhaps the smell of myself would work me up, get me all horny. Make me cum. Yeah, that was now my plan. Let's hope it'd work. I had a creeping dread that it wouldn't, though.

Moments later, and with my doubts still raging, I

rubbed the undies everywhere, inside my armpits, my feet, toes especially, between my butt cheeks, behind my balls, all over them really, and over the length of my dick. It felt nice. Actually, it felt so good I did feel myself stir. Surprise, surprise! I stirred enough to warrant pulling back my foreskin, exposing my knob, to add the smell of that into the mix as well.

And smell the undies did.

They were soon delicately infused with my bodily odors, even if not as strong as I would have liked considering I'd showered this morning. Still. Perhaps it was enough.

I believed I was ready.

Smiling, I lay back proper, my head sinking into my pillow. I brought the undies to my nose with one hand, sniffing deeply, enjoying the delightful tingling sensations I got from doing so.

With my other hand I touched myself. As I did so, running my fingertips over the crown of my quickly swelling knob, feeling my frenulum where the foreskin attached to it as well, so sensitive, so good, that all too familiar sense of me beginning my erotic journey towards climax began.

I writhed.

My movements over myself gained more purpose. I arched my back, sniffing deeper from the undies I held to my nose, a few times replenishing the scents upon them by rubbing them all over myself again.

I did that a few times now that I was working myself up into a sweat. Sweat that was soon mopped up and used to keep me going. Make me hard. 'Cause yeah, believe it or not, and as a surprise to myself, I was fully erect now.

Achingly so.

But that's when something strange happened.

That's when I thought of Larry to spur me on. Our love. Our passionate, wonderful lovemaking. Our special connection 'cause we were meant for each other. I also imagined what I smelled wasn't me at all, but him…no, not him, but his.

As such, the scents became stronger, I swear. More pungent. More manly. Sure, it might be my hopes and dreams working now, but who was I to argue with that?

Pretty much every time I'd jerked off before I'd done things with Larry was either 'cause I'd been watching gay porn or 'cause of my vivid imagination when I couldn't get to my laptop. I mean yeah, before our love was consummated, I'd almost rubbed my foreskin off, circumcising myself, I'm sure, thinking about being with Larry. One day I'd jacked off six times, most during breaks. It would have been more than that, but I had to do *some* work, otherwise my old boss Mister Anderson would have had a coronary. Not a good sight to see that.

But now…now was definitely imagination time.

And did I use such a thing to my full advantage? Hell yeah, I did. I even called out Larry's name many times as I worked myself up into a frenzy. As I stroked myself, harder and faster. As I inhaled deeply the scents that spurred it all on.

A couple more times I had to replenish the odors, but other than that, things went surprisingly well. I was pleased with myself. More so when I felt that all too familiar swirling inside me, emanating from my tightening balls.

A gasp.

A long moan.

A sustained shudder, tingling, numbness at my extremities, then a quick and powerful tremble, a rising of joy that shook me to my core. More shudders, sharp and causing me to gasp. Then, just in the nick of time, I moved so I could unload onto the undies I'd infused with my odors.

One squirt, then two.

Oh, god!

I came and came, a whole body experience for sure.

Three squirts.

Four.

When done, collapsing further into my bed, I squeezed my dick to get out every drop, breathing hard and sweating. The pair of undies I'd soon give to someone who'd help me get my Larry back were now very dirty.

It'd all been worth it.

When dressed, I returned to the lounge room red-faced, still feeling the remnants of my orgasm, breathing deeply. The undies in question in hand, holding them out like they were precious. Which in a way they were.

They'd linked me to Larry for the briefest of moments.

"Here," was all I said as I gave them to Joe, somewhat reluctantly but knowing I had to.

The man smiled in his oily way. "These'll do very nicely." He brought them to his nose. "Ah, I can tell that you've done more than soiled them for me, Jake. How thoughtful of you. How very thoughtful."

"I did what I had to do." I shrugged, going to Dad so I could give him a hug.

He didn't hesitate to embrace me in return. I got the feeling—and I never thought I'd think this in a million years—that he was proud of me for cumming for the man I loved. To save him.

I almost laughed at that. I would have if this whole ridiculous situation wasn't so serious. Wow, what a day already.

Within Dad's hold, I turned to the creep. "Where are they holding my Larry?" I demanded, satisfied I'd kept my end of the agreement.

Joe didn't answer straight away. Instead, he licked some of my jizz from off the undies. "Hmm…very tasty, boy." His smiled turned to one more satisfied. "You're nice and virile, aren't you?"

"Whatever…" was all I offered, shivering uncomfortably that it was someone else enjoying what I'd made, not Larry. "Stop stalling and tell us where Larry is."

Joe looked at Hank.

Hank nodded.

"Alright, seeing as you gave me your special gift, one I shall most certainly cherish." He folded the undies carefully, making sure the thick stringy jizz mess I'd made was inside the folds, protected, before pocketing them. "I'll tell you. There's an old, abandoned winery on the Mornington Peninsula off White Hill Road near the Holmes Road Reserve. You can't miss it. That's where they're keeping him."

Hank immediately said, "Okay, now that's done, let's go, Joe."

The man didn't look surprised though, as if he expected what would happen next. "Yes, I see. Now that I've fulfilled my task, I'm worthless to you, aren't I? I suppose I'll just rot while under police protection now, right?"

"I'm sure you'll be useful again," Hank replied matter-of-factly.

Joe sighed. "Yes, I'm sure, now that I'm officially a snitch."

Hank ignored the man.

To me, Dad, and Tachibana, he said, "If you want to see Larry as much as I do, and know you all do, I suggest we get going as soon as possible."

Dad said incredulous, "Are you serious, Hank? You want us to…to join you? Won't that be dangerous?"

Tachibana agreed.

Hank harrumphed, almost dismissively. "I said you could all come along. I didn't say anything about joining in with the operation, did I? That'll be up to me and a couple of the lads I trust. Okay?"

"I'm still not sure about this, Hank," Dad said, holding me tighter.

"Don't stress. You'll be protected—and once we've got Larry, you'll be able to see him straight away."

Pulling myself out of Dad's hold, I blurted, "Then what are we waiting for?"

But my stomach flipped. I hoped Larry was all right, I really did. We'd come too far, and I'd done things I knew

I'd regret to get the information we needed for it all to go to waste now.

If Larry was alive, that was.

I shook my head, dismissing my spiralling thoughts. I couldn't think like that. It didn't serve any purpose. None at all.

As such, under my breath I said, "Hold on, my big handsome bara man. I'll be with you soon. I promise."

Wednesday Evening, July 28th

Under the cover of a gloomy evening, sky thick with the clouds that'd stuck around all day, we got out of Hank's unmarked car, quickly and quietly. An owl hooted, a dog barked somewhere in the distance, and I got a terrible feeling in my gut.

I stayed close to Dad and Tachibana, nerves rising, my anxiety too. That's when I realized I'd been biting my nails. An old habit come back with a vengeance, it seemed. I shoved my hands into my pockets. Dad put his arm around me. I felt a little better knowing he was here by my side, no matter what happened.

Thankfully, Hank had dropped Joe off a few hours ago; one of Hank's 'lads' taking over from dealing with him. All I could think about was how I was happy I didn't have to sit next to the creep while he was being taken into protection. Wisely, Hank put Joe in the front passenger seat, me between Dad and Tachibana in the back.

I had a sudden urge to get my undies back.

Before I could even ask, a couple of other cars—also unmarked—joined us, headlights turned off before they even stopped. This really was a covert operation, wasn't it?

As soon as the men got out of their vehicles, about six in all, Hank raised his hand, gaining all of our attention.

The men gathered silently, as did the three of us. I swallowed, and heard Dad do the same.

"Okay, listen up, lads," Hank began seriously, his expression more so. "We're going to go in quickly and quietly and do this by the numbers. Got it?"

A chorus of "Yes, sir" resulted.

After that, there was more talk, mostly about how they were going to proceed, in what order they'd do it, what way they'd approach the building, blah, blah, blah. I zoned out. All I was worried about was when Larry would be rescued so I could see him again. Be with him.

Such a thing couldn't happen soon enough in my mind.

Dad, and during a pause in the discussion, always practical, asked, "And what are we to do, Hank?"

"You three stay here out of harm's way." He turned to one of the men closest to him. "Chuck will watch out for you. Right, Chuck?"

Chuck didn't seem too impressed. "Right-o, Sarge." He spat onto the ground as if to emphasize that.

Into the darkness beyond, Hank and his lads disappeared, leaving Chuck to babysit us. Well, that's what I thought, anyway. When they'd gone for a minute or two, minutes that seemed like an eternity, that's when I worried even more. I had to know what was going on.

My patience was wearing thin, truly.

I began pacing—what else could I do? I felt useless. Meanwhile, Dad and Tachibana leant against the bonnet of Hank's car, whispering quietly to themselves. They held hands. I loved how Dad had found someone. I smiled at them, even if it was full of my growing nervousness.

They smiled back.

Chuck suddenly moved to block my path. I looked up at him; he was tall. Really tall. I wouldn't want to get on the bad side of this guy, that's for sure.

Not even looking at me, seemingly disinterested, he said, "I've gotta take a slash. You three going to behave yourselves while I'm gone?"

Dad waved his hand dismissively. "I'm sure we'll manage without you."

Chuck glanced at Dad and Tachibana before I became the target of his attention, his vitriol it turned out. "By the way, which one of you fags wants to come hold my cock for me while I piss, hey? I hear you do that sort of thing, the dirty bastards that you are."

My stomach dropped.

I backed away from the man, unable to form words.

Dad wasn't so silent. "You know, Chuck, I pegged you as a decent sort of guy until you dropped your guard and let your homophobia show. Better watch that, it can leave an ugly stain. One that'll never come off."

Chuck snorted. "So you reckon."

"We are not born with hate, not one of us," Tachibana interjected. "But if we're not careful, it can grow within us due to our ignorance. You are a very ignorant man, officer. Very ignorant."

Chuck turned his back on us, without another word. Okay, he spat onto the ground again, right by my feet, gross! The man trotted off into the bushes on the side of the road.

Good riddance to him.

I hope he never came back.

I was about to go to Dad, rattled somewhat by Chuck's words—no longer trusting the man either, as far as I could throw him—when I heard a gunshot ring out to pierce the still night. Without thinking, heart pounding, I ran.

I ran towards the building where I knew my handsome bara man was being held against his will, as fast as my legs could take me.

I don't know why I ran towards danger, no one or nothing to protect me other than my own stupidity. 'Cause yeah, I was being an idiot, for sure.

But it was too late to turn back now, I reasoned.

Then again, perhaps it was the incident with Chuck that sealed the deal. Yeah, that was it. Definitely. And to be honest, I'd rather face whizzing bullets and desperate members of a gang caught red-handed than spend another moment with a homophobe. I'd gotten enough of that hate from my mum—I shouldn't have to deal with it from a stranger.

Chuck wasn't going to live in my head rent free, no way.

Besides, getting my Larry back was the biggest motivator of them all; I wasn't someone who could sit idly by while the man I loved needed me. I also wasn't someone who wouldn't do whatever it took—within reason—either. I mean, aside from running towards Larry right now, rather recklessly really, my underwear covered in my drying jizz inside Joe's pocket was enough evidence of that, right? *Right?*

With those thoughts, I pushed myself to sprint.

Moments later, I came to a garden wall made of assorted bricks cobbled together.

Breathing hard from my dash, sweat glistening over my exposed arms, I ducked down, hiding behind it. I took a moment to calm. It was then I realized my heart was thumping hard against the back of my ribs. Wow. The adrenalin rush was something else, no lie.

My head went all cotton wool fuzzy too.

Another moment of waiting before I gathered up the balls to run towards my next goal, a shed where the winery must have once kept its equipment, tractors and the like, no doubt, I realized I'd been hasty in my decision. Again…too late now. I was out here; might as well keep going.

I sucked in a breath, one that steeled my resolve. I got up, bounded over the wall, and ran. Ran until my pounding heart gave me that rush again. That hit.

Exhilarating, for sure.

But as I came to full stride, another gunshot rang out. *Bang!* God, it sounded so close. I ducked immediately behind a bush. Not much protection I knew, but hopefully in the growing darkness no one saw me.

I heard shouting.

Slowly, I crawled on my hands and knees towards the shed, sweating, stomach tight, keeping as low as I could. Or, more the point, so I didn't attract any unwanted attention. 'Cause yeah, that wouldn't be great right about now.

Not ever, truthfully.

I made it, even though it took me forever…well, it seemed that way, especially considering the ground wasn't exactly the best surface, all sharp stones, twigs, and grass burrs. My hands and knees would be cut to pieces, I knew. Still. It was a small price to pay to get Larry back, my comfort unimportant.

He'd be a lot worse than a few scratches on him, no damn doubt.

Once I got to the shed, again I had to catch my breath. Compose myself. Pluck up the courage to go on. But I had to get even closer than what I'd already achieved by some miracle.

I looked around; there wasn't much cover.

To the left, under large swaying trees from a gentle breeze that'd kicked up, there were numerous cars. Ones belonging to the crooks, I'd say. To the right, there was nothing at all other than an open field where the grapes used to grow in neat rows. That was now weed-infested. I didn't want to go there.

Ahead, that's where the main building was, where all the commotion came from. I didn't think the direct route was viable. No cover between me and my goal. None at all.

I decided to run for the cars, the best option considering I didn't have time to waste, every moment I delayed was a moment Larry might not have. Although, thinking about such things further, what was I going to do when I got to him…*if* I got to him? Use foul language against the bad guys? Flash my butt to give them an eyeful of my recently fucked hole thanks to the hotel room intimacy me and Larry shared the other night?

Yeah, that'd make them all drop their guns and surrender—not! I therefore decided I'd play things by ear, ignore my nagging doubts before they spiralled out of control. It had gotten me this far, why not further?

I stood, bolting towards my newest goal.

As I did so, already feeling the ache in my muscles 'cause of the rush, through my legs especially, the front door to the winery's main building slammed open, clattering against the brickwork. Streaming light from within the building blinded me. I shielded my eyes.

"What the fuck are you doing here, Jake?!" I heard Hank yell. "Get your ass outta here! Now!"

Another gunshot sounded, that time deafening.

I put down my hand after ducking instinctively. I was trembling I realized, as reality suddenly hit me like a cold slap to the face. I was in danger!

Oh, fuck!

Before I could do as Hank commanded, that's when I saw him. That's when my gaze fell upon Larry. My Larry. I gasped, aching all over, the pain of being so close to him yet so far overwhelming me above everything else. I wanted to hold Larry, comfort him.

And the worst part was I knew I couldn't.

Larry was injured. Badly. He was also being supported by Hank around his waist, obviously unable to walk of his own accord.

More pain coursed through me.

Larry didn't look good, his head was hung low,

swaying, shoulders slumped, body too, as Hank ran as best he could, gait awkward, being so burdened.

Without thought I ran towards them, wanting to help. Again, and in hindsight, that probably wasn't one of the better ideas I'd been blessed with lately.

Once more there was gunfire, that time a few shots in a row.

After placing Larry onto the ground, quick as anything, Hank charged at me, colliding into me seconds later. I yelped, finding myself without air in my lungs and his weight pressed upon me, the hard dirt against my back. I'd been tackled to the ground.

"Ouch!" was all I managed once I could breathe again…sort of.

"You bloody idiot!" Hank scolded. "What do you think's going to happen now that I've got two of you to save now, hmm? As if there wasn't enough to worry about here."

"I'm…s-sorry."

"Don't be sorry," he spat. "Just do as you're told, or I'll—"

More shots interrupted Hank's reprimand. He quickly ducked his head while coming closer to me, our lips almost touching. I winced, fear and anxiety striking me harder. But before I could tell him to give me some space, he'd got up off me and was back helping Larry.

A relief.

To me, eyes wild with anger, glaring daggers at me really, Hank added, "If you're going to be a disobedient pain in the ass, Jake, you might as well make yourself useful and come over here and help me. Your boyfriend weights a tonne!"

"O…okay," I said weakly, feeling the heat of his words burning my embarrassed cheeks further.

I clambered up to an awkward stand, not bothering to dust myself off, also trying to avoid any wayward bullets as best I could. If I failed, I'd be dead, although my only concern was getting to Larry, my man drifting out of conscious from the look of it.

Hank helped me carry Larry when I got to my goal. From there, we made it to the cover of the cars without incident, hiding as best we could behind the biggest, a sleek black Mercedes I recognized.

"Stay here," Hank commanded, gruffly. "Whatever you do, don't move. But above all, for the love of God, don't draw any attention to yourself. I'll be back in a minute—the lads need me."

Before I could protest, even beg for him to stay, Hank left us. I couldn't believe it. Just like that, he was gone. My heart pounded even more as my fears grew beyond anything I'd imagined before. Sure, I had Larry with me, but what use was that if we were still in danger and unable to defend ourselves?

None, right?

At that moment, distracting me from the unfolding drama around me, Larry coughed. He then moaned in pain, holding his head. I moved to hold him, bring him close to me, cradling him in my arms as he would to me if the situation were reversed.

I became emotional, tears welling.

"It's me, Larry, your Jake-y boy," I said as reassuringly as I could muster considering I was shitting bricks 'cause the gunfire was getting worse ever since Hank had left us.

I also heard shouting, swearing, and yells of both agony and defiance from many voices. Again, close. Too close.

More gunfire.

"Whaaat?" Larry mumbled.

I kissed his forehead with trembling lips, tasting blood from off his skin where he'd been hit or whatever while captured by the gang. I didn't want to think about that, though. He was alive, and that's all that mattered.

"It's Jake-y, Larry." I ran my hand over his cheek tenderly. "Your Jake-y."

A roll of his eyes as he looked up at me. "Jake-y?" There was a glimmer of recognition there.

A hope.

My heart fluttered, all for him.

"Yeah, that's right. It's me. It's your Jake-y. I'm here to get you outta here, I promise. Just hold on, okay?"

Larry didn't answer but nodded, grabbing my hand to hold it for a moment before letting go. I took that as his understanding. He looked exhausted—what had he been through? I couldn't even begin to imagine.

My heart ached for him.

I tried to stand, pull him up at the same time, but it was no use. Larry was a big man. My big handsome bara man. And yeah, I wouldn't have it any other way, but right now I needed *him* to help *me* help him. I couldn't do it on my own.

"Can you stand?" I asked, lips trembling, fear becoming

as intense as the battle going on around us—I even smelt the acrid tang of gun smoke.

Not good. Not good at all.

Larry moved…slowly.

It was painful to witness. He was hurt. Hurt beyond belief, I knew it. Tears then did fall; I became so overcome seeing him like that. But I didn't get time to wipe them away, 'cause that's when I felt something cold and hard being pressed against my back between my shoulder blades.

No prizes for guessing what it was—I'd felt it before at my temples not that long ago.

A colder and harder voice said, "Look what we have here, a pretty boy trying to be a hero, huh?"

I didn't reply. What could I say? "Oh hey, yeah, I'm just going to sneak outta here with my boyfriend so we can be witnesses to what you've done here. I hope you don't mind." Obviously not.

Instead, I froze, looking down at Larry, tears falling. Tears of my failure. Tears for him. For myself too, knowing we would never have a life together beyond that amazing night at the hotel room. Sure, it may have been only one night, but to me it was everything. The universe lived and breathed in those moments between us. They were magical.

I wouldn't swap anything I did for nothing, not even the stupid stuff to get me to this point. At least I would go with Larry in my arms. By my side. Together.

My heart sank as the man pressed the gun harder into me. "How about I shoot your boyfriend first, pretty boy?" he said, sneering even more, clearly enjoying the power he held over us 'cause he held a weapon. "I like the idea of making you watch him die before I plug you. Gives me a thrill right to my balls, it does. Turns me on."

With the specter of death standing behind me, breathing down my neck as it were, time seemed to stop. It didn't, of course. That was silly. Instead, I realized my consciousness had taken me out of the moment, my thoughts wandering to a few weeks ago, back to the time when I'd first set my eyes on Larry.

That day wasn't even a nice one. Dreary, early winter cold. Freezing too. I was rugged up worse than a newbie holidaymaker at the Mt. Bulla snowfields, truly. I was still cold.

Good thing I was heading for the local gym, 'cause perving on all the sexy bara men, their bulging muscles glistening with sweat, so hot, while I did my thing on the treadmill would get me warmed up soon enough.

Really warm.

Going into the place, the glass entrance door covered in promotional posters, fitness schedules, and adverts for sports drinks was blocked by the biggest man I'd ever seen. Like huge, he was! Over six feet tall and with muscles most bodybuilders would sell their souls for, their first born thrown in too.

"Um…excuse me please, but I need to get through," I said weakly within the man's shadow; I dare not touch him, he may take offence and then he'd just break me by flexing his eyebrows or something.

The man turned towards me…slowly.

As soon as our eyes met, and I know this sounds so god-awfully cringe-y, but that's when something happened. Something special. Not sparks, but a connection, like the threads that made up existence weaved us together in that moment. I'd never felt anything like it. 'Cause not only did I suck in a deep breath, I got all weak kneed too. Went all funny.

Everywhere.

So much so, I soon found myself in his arms, our gaze close, noses almost touching. I even got that whole stomach fluttering with butterflies happening then. I'd never felt like that with anyone. Not on first sight, anyway. What a topsy-turvy, wonderful rush!

The mountain of a man said smoothly, "I suppose now that I've found myself holdin' ya, we'd better introduce ourselves. I'm Larry. Larry Olsen. And you are?"

"Larry?" My head was a spin, a wonderfully confusing bewildering spin.

"Yeah, Larry. That's my name." His expression softened. "What's yours?"

"Jake…" I couldn't remember my surname all of a sudden; I was so taken in by him.

Larry's expression turned to happiness, a beautiful smile, one that went to my heart and hadn't vacated it since. "Jake, huh! Ya wanna hot drink or somethin'? I'll buy."

"Sure, but I'm—jeez, you smell so good." I flushed with heat, realising I'd said that out loud, 'cause yeah, I loved his musky-woody scent with cinnamon and sweet as sugar undertones. "Er…sure, I'd like to have a drink with you."

He held his gaze, as I did mine. I hadn't looked away

from him since that day either. Not literally, but with the connection we created since our first meeting. One that never broke. And it was then I realized I'd do anything required to keep that feeling. I'd even risk my life for Larry. 'Cause what was life without love? True love?

As such, I came back to myself.

Back to the terrible moment.

But I wasn't scared anymore. Love had made me stronger. So strong I pulsed with it, could feel it twisting inside me, spurring me on. It also made me someone special to someone else. 'Cause yeah, I was Larry's someone special, as he was special to me. And really, what could go against that? Nothing. Nothing could destroy our love.

With the gun moved so it no longer pressed against my back, the man obviously wanted to enact his threat, that's when I took the opportunity to do what I had to. To protect my Larry. To save *us* too.

Keep our connection, no matter what.

With a blindingly fast turn, as best I could manage, anyway, I spun on my heels to face my attacker. But I didn't face him completely. No. I only turned enough to get to his outstretched arm, the arm that held the gun, the threat to me and to Larry.

Without thought, pure instinct really, and with everything a blur as my love for Larry fuelled my movements, spurred me on, I chopped at the man's wrist with my clenched tight, knuckles white, fist.

A yelp from him as he dropped the weapon, surprise etched onto his otherwise ugly face. I didn't care if I hurt him or not, so long as he didn't hurt us. Not ever.

When the gun fell to the ground, I kicked it away.

That's when I also brought my knee up into his groin. If I'd stopped and thought about what I did, it never would have happened, no way. What I did was so unlike me. But yeah, my actions were now purely motivated by instinct and self-preservation, no doubt. Also, my protective instincts towards Larry as well, 'cause he couldn't do it himself being so injured after what these bastards had done to him.

In truth, I just wanted this to be over and done with.

To my fortune, it seemed the universe—or that connection between Larry and me—must have been looking out for us in those moments. My knee connected perfectly within that vulnerable spot between his legs.

An "Oof" from the crook resulted, a double over, a gasping for air like a fish out of water, clutching himself, before he went down like a sack of spuds dropped from a height.

The man hit the dirt with a wonderful *thud!*

But I didn't have time to congratulate myself. I had to get Larry outta here. Going to him, seeing him up close for the first time, my worry increased ten-fold. Without putting it any other way, he'd been beaten up, bruises all over him, some already purpling. No doubt he had broken ribs too.

The fucking bastards.

I wanted to kill them all.

I had no time to do anything, not even get Larry to his feet again, worry consuming me, 'cause the guy I kneed in his balls had somehow recovered already. Were they bloody well made of steel?

Just my luck to try and tangle with a steel-balled crook if they were.

He grabbed me. I shouted in protest, in pain too, as his hands gripped my shoulders. Then, with violent force, I was pulled away, the action knocking me on my ass.

The man spat, "I'm going to enjoy killing you, boy."

I don't know why, but I goaded, "Yeah, you don't even have a gun! How're you going to do that?"

"Like this!" And with that, he struck at me with a karate chop-style hit, one that connected with the soft spot at the top of my shoulders.

Pain shot through me.

Holy fuck did pain shoot through me. What did he do? Hit a pressure point or something. Jeez, I reeled. I also yelped, instinctively holding where he'd struck me.

And that's when I was left vulnerable.

Taking the opportunity of my moment of weakness, the man punched me in the opposite side, right in my kidneys. I staggered, thankfully the Mercedes at my back stopped my fall even if I thudded into it, losing my breath once more. More pain. Fuck!

My shoulder still hurt, but nowhere near as much as my side did. Tears welled. Tears of pain combined with the feelings of worry I had for Larry.

I understood how this man was going to kill me without his gun. Something he'd accomplish with his bare hands, he was that good. So much so, not only were his fists deadly weapons against me while I was disorientated and searing with pain, head spinning even more, he kicked me.

Fucking hell!

It was one of those mixed martial arts style kicks, roundhouse and striking me once more on my side, higher up to wind me. And wind me it did. It also knocked me onto my ass beside Larry.

"Jake-y, ya there…?" my man said with a slur, one where he was no doubt drunk with pain—as I was.

I tried to stagger up.

What got me to my feet weren't my own efforts. No. The man, my attacker hell bent on ending me, picked me up like I was nothing. Sure, I was a skinny twink, only about five and a half foot in height, less than sixty-five kilos in weight, but hey, this was getting ridiculous.

I was nothing to him in more ways than one, I realized.

As soon as he pulled me up to his height, he spat, "Say your prayers, boy. This will soon be over."

In that moment, I couldn't think of anything else to do but spit in his eye, so I did. I hocked a thick gob, all stringy and green-tinged. I was damn proud of it. Truly.

Of course, the bastard didn't share my sentiments.

He dropped me. That time, I didn't fall. I stayed standing. In the moment where he was defenceless this time, I punched him in his stomach as hard as I could. God, my hand hurt when I connected.

To both my surprise and disappointment, he must have been expecting my move. He'd tightened his muscles there. No wonder it hurt me and not him.

"Nice try." He'd finished wiping his face of my saliva. "But it won't get you very far."

And that's when he went into full-on rage mode, me the target. I was kicked and punched, his hands and feet moving quick as lightning. That time I wasn't only stunned, in agony too, I was once more on the floor, holding myself, wanting it to be over with.

I failed my man.

Failed myself too.

With greater tears welling, breathless, shuddering in pain, I tried to stagger to my feet. My legs and arms didn't want to cooperate with what my fuzzy head wanted them to do. I didn't get much of a chance to do anything, let alone defend myself.

He kicked me again.

I yelled. Then he kept kicking. Over and over, not giving me the chance to do anything but scream in agony at being attacked with such precision and devastation.

I was so out of my league it wasn't funny.

What was I thinking? Talk about delusional, or what. How I'd even thought I could take on anyone, let alone a guy twice my age and way more experienced at doing shit like this than what I'd ever be was anyone's guess.

I certainly had no clue, did I?

Another kick hit me, connected just so, right where my ribs met with the softer part of my stomach. That time the air was definitely knocked from me. I heaved, trying to get air into my lungs, failing miserably. Argh! I was done for!

On all fours, managing that at least, saliva slobbered from mouth, spitting, cursing, and wishing I wasn't such a weakling, I could feel my tears fall as much as my hopes of getting out of this situation alive.

"Stand up, boy. Face me like a man. C'mon, the fun's only just begun."

To defy him I wanted to run. Simply get as far away as possible. But I couldn't do that. I could never leave Larry. Not ever. With wobbling arms, still coughing and spluttering, aching all over, more so where I was kicked, I managed to stand.

"Do your worst," I spat.

"Gladly!" And with that one word, full of hate and poison, he clenched his fist, about to take a swing at me.

That's when I heard a gunshot.

Bang!

I almost jumped out of my skin; it was that close. In fact, I did. I shielded myself as best I could as I ducked. But what I saw was something I'd never forget for as long as I'd live.

The man had been shot, right in the chest, blood blossoming from it like an opening red rose greeting the approaching morning. A gasp. A gurgle from him. He spat blood, shocked.

He then slumped to the ground, dead.

I couldn't believe it. I turned to Larry, shocked. Shocked to my bones. That's when I saw him, my handsome bara man, holding the smoking weapon.

With a drawl, he said, "He was givin' me…the shits, that one."

"Larry!" I didn't know whether to cheer or what.

But before I could do anything, he had returned to the world of the unconscious, dropping the gun in the process. Without another heartbeat, I rushed to him, holding him tightly.

Seemed my man, despite his injuries and what they did to him, had saved me.

I was fine with that.

Damn bloody fine.

Hank and the lads quickly got the situation under control after that. I kept a hold of Larry until help arrived, comforting him, whispering that I was there for him, always. What else could I do? I couldn't carry him. Not a chance. But I could stay with him.

Just as good, right?

While the gang was being herded up, made to lie on the ground, hands behind their back, handcuffed, Hank approached, a victorious smirk planted on his lips.

"It's over." He looked down at the dead man Larry had shot. "What happened here?"

I looked between the dead body and Hank. "Self-defence," was all I offered.

Hank simply nodded.

The sound of a car, actually many cars, all cop cars—sirens wailing—approaching took over everything else. Hank had obviously called for backup. It had arrived. Good timing—not.

Where was it ten minutes ago when I needed help before having the ever-loving crap beaten out of me? I couldn't bloody move now other than to comfort Larry as much as I tried to comfort myself.

"This isn't over!" one of the crooks said, spittle flying as he was taken away by two of Hank's lads, then bundled into the backseat of the nearest cop car. "Mister Yaketsuku's boys will get you. Get you all!" The man glared at Hank when he yelled that last part.

"Take the bastards away!" Hank shot back.

I never wanted to see any of those crooks ever again. Something told me this wasn't over, though. Maybe for Larry and me, hopefully, but certainly not for Hank.

Certainly not.

I also had a feeling he'd have a lot of explaining to do. I didn't envy him, not one bit.

Monday, August 9th

Finally, *finally* we were home after that fateful night and the resulting hospital stay for Larry. Yeah, I was checked over—nothing serious other than a couple of cracked ribs and plenty of bruises—but it was his injuries which were far more serious. Way more, in fact. More than I could have imagined.

He was bleeding internally, needing surgery.

When we were discharged, Dad and Tachibana joining us, fussing over the both of us, being parents really, bless them, Larry seemed distant.

"What's the matter?" I asked.

He looked at me, moving so he held my hand, the both of us walking out of the hospital holding each other. It was like a dream. A wonderful, beautiful romantic dream. I loved it.

"Nothin's wrong…but I want ya to live with me, Jake-y. Be with me always. I need ya; recent events have made it clear I can't do it all alone."

Without hesitation I replied, "I need you too. And hell yeah, when can I bring my stuff over to your apartment? 'Cause I'm there!"

"Now."

"Then now it'll be."

• • •

I moved in.

Larry's apartment wasn't huge, or to be more precise, neither was his bedroom…correction, our bedroom. It only had a bed, chest of drawers, a tall boy, and not much else within. But hey, considering what was going to happen in there now that I was settled, in this case size didn't matter.

The only size I cared about was Larry's—in every way. 'Cause yeah, his big, beautiful bulk was draped over our double bed lazily as he watched me unpack the last of my things into the chest of drawers, my numerous undies and socks.

I then snuggled up to him, close as I could get, my leg over him to really claim him as mine. For the longest moment, I just looked at my man lovingly, smiling, feeling warm and gooey inside knowing that he was safe. Safe with me. I also felt comforted by being in his big, strong arms once more as a couple. As we should be. This was how the universe was meant to be. Full of love.

Hope too.

'Cause yeah, I now had both in equal measure.

He whispered, "Get ya clothes off, Jake-y…I wanna make you even hotter for me than I know ya already are."

I giggled. "I'm already as hot as I can get for you." I ran my hand down his arm, my fingers feeling the delightful tension in his massive muscles.

So sexy.

He grinned widely. "In that case, I wanna make you cum."

"That I can so do for you; give you heaps too." I kissed his arm, moving my attention towards his lips via the long route across his massive pecs and all over his neck to get to them. "But what happened to romance, hey?"

"What'd'ya mean?"

I licked his lower lip, my tongue infused with the scents of my journey over him, wet trails across his heated skin in my wake, feeling myself as hard as ever.

"You could have said you want to make love to me," I replied.

An eyebrow rose. "Love is what happens between us within every moment, whether we're awake or asleep. To say we're gonna 'make love' gives it a boundary. I don't want that, 'cause that's not how I feel 'bout ya. Not at all."

I got that lovely hitch in my throat, the fluttering tummy thing too. "That's…beautiful." And it was, truly. "What would you call it, our moments of physical love, then?"

He shrugged one shoulder only. "Why can't we call it what it is? We're gonna fuck. Nothin' complicated or fancy 'bout that, is there? Sounds dead sexier too!"

I had to agree with him. "No…you're right." I kissed him again and again, tasting him, aching for him. "Let's fuck before I go outta my mind!"

"Hell yeah! It's been too long."

"It so has," I replied, the lovely fluttering built up to quivering, overtaking me as I moved so I could shed my clothing for my man, his eyes widening as I did so.

I was his.

Always.

I was also as hard as ever, my dick throbbing all for him, my body too. And from that moment on, everything was perfect. 'Cause while we looked into each other's eyes, neither of us losing that connection, not even when I sucked…no worshipped, his dick, really getting my saliva dribbling all over him, lubricating him, tasting him, smelling him, oh god what a turn on, I then rode his nine-incher like it was an important part of me that'd been missing for so long.

Which it had been.

To have him inside me, yeah, painful at first like always, but when things settled, when my love and feelings for him overtook everything else, I became more comfortable.

Even more in love.

"You're so good, Jake-y."

Getting heated, feeling myself climb the heights with each hard thrust of his dick, I managed, "I…I do my b-best for you."

He began thrusting upwards with more intent. I was gasping, intoxicated, holy fuck how I needed this. So, so much! Wow! As such, I moved my ass, kind of twerking it so I could feel every inch of him moving within me, rubbing me in all the right places, making me leak, the lip of my un-retracted foreskin stretched over my swollen knob, wet and glistening.

My dick dribbled onto his abs, forming a little wet spot. A stain on his tanned, rippling-with-muscles stomach. My stain. I liked that idea. I liked it so much it made me even hornier. Made me shudder. Made me moan and groan, saliva dripping from my open mouth.

Larry was soon covered in sweat.

I could smell him, his heat, his manliness even more, rising from him to soak into me, loving it. Jeez, I was overwhelmed. It was his stain upon me, marking me as his. Always. I became even more immersed in him when he moved his hands so he could hold my hips, push me down further onto his dick, seating me fully.

"You're so…deep!" I whimpered, eyes watering, feeling like he was splitting me in two.

I loved it.

"I'm not gonna last, Jake-y! I'm not—" And before he could even finish his words, that's when Larry, my big handsome bara man, gave me all of what he could give.

He shuddered, bucking me. Good thing he held my hips, I'd have been flung off him, ass on the floor, legs open and my gaping hole empty. I needed it filled. And boy, did Larry fill it.

He came and came.

The sensation of it, the thought of how his jizz was now deep in my gut, becoming a part of me, his proteins absorbed by my body to give me even more strength, mark me on the inside, the thought of it tipping me over the edge too.

That feeling, right inside my balls, deeper than that really, spread quickly to consume me. I groaned. Shouted my joy. I then blew my load, hands free, while still taking Larry's.

It was the most mind-blowing orgasm I'd ever had. I went numb and tingly all at the same time. Tingly-numb? Was that a thing? Holy fucking hell, one thing was certain,

I was transported into a sort of limbo place, one that was drenched in our love.

I never wanted to leave it.

"Oh, my fucking god…you made m-me cum from…from my ass!" I stammered, still shuddering, heated, flushed, and my head spinning as I began the descent from my heavenly heights.

It was unlike anything I'd felt before. Simply wow! And what's more, Larry's dick was *still* inside me, rubbing against my now hypersensitive prostate. I hadn't gone flaccid, as rock hard as ever even after covering Larry with my love in thick ribbons to his chin, his abs and massive pecs drenched most of all.

Fucking awesome!

"No lyin', ya came a hella lot, Jake-y!" Larry said breathing hard and sweating…no glistening, dripping really. He let go of me so he could dip his fingers into my cum, taste me, savor it.

So good to see that.

"I needed you so bad—and I love seeing you wear my jizz."

Larry chuckled. "Pretties me up a bit, does it?"

"It does. And after I lick up my mess, do you want to go again?" I smiled, feeling my thirst rising for my man already, my dick dripping my intentions even more, cum and pre-cum mixed to stain his skin even more.

"Do I love ya?"

"You sure do."

"Then there's only one answer, ain't there?"

"There is."

I collapsed into Larry's arms. We kissed, tongues and giddiness and all. I loved him so much. And the biggest blessing of all was that Larry seemed to be a lot better after his ordeal, back to his old self more so.

Then again, nothing heals like love.

And a good fucking as well!

Friday, August 14th
(Epilogue)

We stayed in each other's arms, loving each other, fucking whenever we could, cumming, laughing, living, and just being, for the rest of the week. Just recharging ourselves before we got on with life. Returned to work or whatever.

"We should go out tonight," I said on Friday morning, sun struggling to peek through the clouds outside, running my hand over Larry's morning wood, getting him harder.

"Oh…where?"

"My cousin Rion messaged me yesterday," I explained. "He wants to go on a double date—check out the sushi bars around, you know, dinner and sake, that sort of thing. Should be fun."

Larry scrunched up his face. "I don't know if I wanna go out with a straight couple in tow. Cramp my style, won't it?"

"Your style is your hands all over my butt." I snorted a laugh. "But don't worry, my cousin's gay." Larry seemed to relax. Jeez, he was adorable, such a soft and gentle giant, unbelievable it was. I wouldn't have it any other way either. "He's got a new boyfriend, so yeah I suppose he wants to introduce him to us all."

"Okay, then."

"Good. I'll let Rion know we're going—our first official date, I believe. Right?"

Larry's eyebrows rose. "Ya right. I mean, before now we were too busy fucking to bother going out."

"And aren't I glad for that." I kissed him; he returned it, wanting it to go deeper, obviously needing our tongues to connect. I pulled away teasingly. "Very glad."

He grabbed me, his touch wandering between my butt cheeks so he could rub his attention over my hole in little circles, sending shivers of delight all through me to then settle at the base of my spine.

I moaned my approval.

Because of that, his affection most of all, I quickly succumb to him. His touch got more intense, more teasing too. After he'd stimulated me, got me hard and leaking for him, he wrapped his big, strong arms around me, engulfing me, pulling me closer. I gave him what he wanted. My tongue, my body, and my ass.

It's what I wanted too, no doubt.

The bar, a place called *Kanpai Japanese Sushi Bar &* *Grill*, where we were to meet Rion and his new boyfriend—Tetsu his name—was a lovely place, all full of ambiance and the hallmarks of Japanese culture. There was even a cherry blossom tree, a live one, in the middle of the eating area.

It also helped the door greeter was cute.

Larry gave me a side eye but also smiled cheekily when he caught me checking out the guy's butt as he led us to Rion and Tetsu's table, menus in hand.

I offered in defence, "Hey, I can smell the roses, so long as I don't pick them, right?"

"Don't gimme that guff," he replied. "I know what happens when ya start smellin' things." He laughed gently, at the same time he held my hand tighter.

"Fair point." I moved closer to him so I was brushing against his bulk, walking in his shadow where I belonged and where I loved being. "Can I smell you after dinner, then?"

"I got my special combination cologne prepared just for that."

I then had a thought. "Can you…like not spritz yourself with it too much? I love your more *natural* odors. They get me horned up so badly, I love it. Especially when they're all over me too."

"Ya a dirty boy, Jake-y."

"You wouldn't have it any other way, would you?"

"Not a fuckin' chance."

Rion was as I remembered him, a shock of red hair his most prominent feature. He was naturally a ginger, but I think he dyed it to accentuate it. He looked good.

His boyfriend though, now he was something else. If he were a takeaway, he'd be finger licking good. Dark haired like raven's feathers, soft features, thick lips and eyebrows—such nice eyebrows—and wearing trendy glasses too, the top of them frameless. Even Larry was taken aback, his hold on me gripping even tighter now.

Rion stood as soon as he saw us approach, all lean and tall and as cute as ever. "Hey guys, allow me to introduce Tetsu—my boyfriend."

There were handshakes all round.

"And this is my handsome man, Larry," I said.

More handshakes, smiles, and warmth. Once the pleasantries were over, we sat once our escort handed us the menus, declaring he'd return soon once we'd made our choices.

When we got it, the meal was excellent, I had to say.

I had the okonomiyaki, a dinner inside an omelette, so good! Larry had the same. I tried a couple of the sushi too. By the time we'd eaten, drank our fill of saké as well, Rion and Tetsu kissed each other. A gentle touch of lips, so adorable.

We soon ordered dessert.

It was then, while the wagashi and green tea was presented, impeccably so, looking tasty, I realized I hadn't kissed Larry in public. Not yet. A situation I'd soon rectify, no doubt. And seeing as we were in the gayer friendly part of town, I didn't see why I couldn't.

So, I did.

I kissed him with all the love and desire I could muster—which wasn't hard. Well, *that* was hard…but as for the rest of my feelings, they were a given. I loved him.

Simple as that.

When we parted, my head in a lovely spin, Rion said, "Aww, you two are great together."

"As are you and Tetsu," I replied.

Rion drained his green tea. "Say, you want to go to another bar, one a bit more adult?"

I looked at Larry, sensing his need to be alone with me

after this. "Sorry, but we have other plans. Maybe next time."

Rion looked between us. "Yeah, I get it." He winked his understanding.

Larry blushed. "I can't help it Jake-y gives me a boner I need him to see to, can I?"

We all laughed.

After that, and paying our bills, splitting it so it was even between us all, Rion and Tetsu left, no doubt to continue their night out. I was glad Larry only wanted me and me alone. I needed him as much as he needed me, truly.

"They were great together, weren't they?" I said, running my hand over his leg, moving it towards my intention, feeling his bulge. He was as hard as my lust. Wow.

"They were."

"But can we do one more thing before we leave?"

"What's that?"

I felt heat wash all through me. "Can I suck your dick in the toilets? I've always wanted to do that, and seeing as you're my man, I want to do that with you. Get risky and frisky, I mean."

Larry was standing before I could blink. "Ya *are* a dirty boy."

"I'm your dirty boy, no lie."

He grabbed my hand. "Then let's go, 'fore I blow in my jocks and you'll get it second hand not direct."

"Oh, I'll get it direct."

"How can ya be sure? Ya been makin' me horny all night, what with ya touchin' and ya eyes devourin' me."

I smiled, right to my soul where our connection lived in an eternal bliss. "I can get you worked up twice. Do whatever it takes so it happens too."

Larry's eyes widened. "Fuck, Jake-y, I love ya so much."

"I love you too."

Suffice it to say, getting my second desert, all bitter and salty and hot down my throat, topped off our first date perfectly. And yeah, I blew him twice while in the restaurant's toilets—the cubicles big enough for us both to do our thing. How considerate of them to make them like that. I was such a greedy boy, wasn't I? Dirty too.

My man gave no complaints.

That night Larry fucked me, hard. Over and over. So fucking hard, I saw stars within the wheeling heavens every time he got deep inside me, gasping, me gagging for more. I also came all over his muscles and face hands free one of those times, thick ribbons of it too. I didn't need my hands when my man's dick touched me in all the right places, did I?

And besides, come to think of it, I didn't need anything but his love, as I loved him.

What else mattered?

Nothing.

Nothing at all.

The End

Author's Note

A 'bara' is a man with lots of muscles—think body builder. Also, I hoped you enjoyed the second part of this quadrilogy, concluding over the next two books, *Catching Two Frogs with One Hand* and *The Chirping Cricket Desires the Ripened Crop*.

Thanks for reading!

About the Author

By day I'm a humble physical therapist...and by day I'm also a writer of sweet & saucy boyslove stories (18+). I sleep at night as an old fart like me should. I'm both self-published and traditionally published. Other than that, I live with my partner and two cats and live my best life.

Website: http://konblackeboyslovewriter.com

Twitter: http://www.twitter.com/blackekon

Also by Kon Blacke
Published by Dreamsphere Books

Immortal Whispers
Kon Blacke

The Whispering Monks have foretold change to the world, and it's fast approaching. They also speak of the mortals who'll be involved.

Hereward, a lord knight who only worships the steel at his side, as the mad magician Ealdræd has taken away everyone he had ever loved. Wymond, an oblate determined to find his true self, even if it means turning away from everything he has ever known. Beornræd, a powerful magician who fears to love again after the cruelties of his past. Kieron, a stable hand with dragon blood flowing through his veins and is the rightful heir to a realm of unimaginable beauty.

All four will travel their own paths, to destroy their pasts and rebuild their future, as they thwart the evil plans of Ealdræd and his conduit, the immortal Abbot Hosho.

The whisperings continue through epic battles, both on the ground and in the sky.

The whisperings shall continue beyond the aftermath.

As it has been foretold.

More from Deep Desires Press

The Hookups of Hickeyhook Hall
Marco May

Jenner is gay and has a crush on Michael. Unbeknownst to him, Michael is bi and has a crush on him in return. But there's one huge obstacle in the way of professing his love. Their parents just got married to each other. Now, they're officially stepbrothers.

Both young men are determined to move on and leave their feelings behind, and what better way to do that than to dive into the challenges of starting a new life at Hickeyhook College? Their new lives are full of quirky roommates and stupid rules...and the discovery of an underground sex club with both students and staff that offers students the opportunity to cheat their way through to graduation without all the stresses of normal college life. With both young men in the club, it brings Jenner and Michael dangerously close, making it impossible to ignore the feelings they both swore to leave behind.

As sticky as their new situation is, it's about to get stickier. The powerful Dean Wicket sees the emerging relationship between Jenner and Michael and he's determined to get in the way...because he wants Michael to himself.

When the truth of Jenner and Michael comes out and the world is against them, these two men must fight with all they have to hold onto true love.